SWEET SUBMISSION

by

LIA ANDERSSEN

Published by **CHIMERA**
ISBN 9781901388671

Chapter 1

The lovely peasant girl crouched in the undergrowth, scarcely breathing as she listened hard for the sound of pursuers. Amid the beautiful tranquillity of the forest, it scarcely seemed possible that evil could be lurking there. The sun shone down through the trees from a clear blue sky, and all about her birds were singing. Yet it seemed a strange and fearsome place to the youngster as she peered about.

She cupped her ear and cocked her pretty head to one side. The silence that surrounded her gave her unexpected hope. Perhaps she had actually shaken them off. Perhaps the twisted and tortured path she had taken through the undergrowth, with the thorns and prickles scratching at her bare legs, had done the trick. Perhaps she was safe, after all.

In her heart, though, she doubted it. The men who were chasing her were practised hunters all, and were well used to tracking their prey across the dense terrain in which she found herself. Experience told her that it would only be a matter of time before they were up with her again.

Belita cursed her stupidity in taking the shortcut back to her village. It shaved more than three miles from the journey, no small distance when on foot, but she had been warned time and time again about the dangers of the forest, and of the men who lived there. Now, too late, she realised that they had been no idle warnings.

The men had come across her when she least expected to meet them. She had been hurrying along, intent on getting home as soon as possible, when she found herself suddenly stumbling out of the shelter of the trees and into an open clearing. They had been standing on the far side of the grassy area.

She had no more than a few seconds to observe the small band as she pulled up sharply, recognising them at once as a hunting party. The forest was full of wild boar, which provided a plentiful and cheap food for the forest dwellers. The way the men were dressed and armed told her at once that their quarry was food. The sight of the lovely village girl had diverted their attention from their task, however, and she knew they had quite another prey in mind as they began to run towards her, laughing and shouting to one another.

Belita had turned and run at once, careering back and forth through the trees as the men pursued her. Since her childhood she had been told of the cruelty of the forest dwellers, and she knew she was in danger. These people would have no pity on a village girl, and she had few doubts what they would do if they caught her.

Her youthfulness and fitness served her well during the initial pursuit, but she had run blindly from her pursuers. Now, as she crouched gasping for breath, she tried to get her bearings once more. She knew the village was to the west, and the position of the afternoon sun gave her a good idea in which direction she should be heading, but she was only too aware that the forest men knew every inch of this area, and were skilled at tracking their prey. If she were to stand any chance at all of escaping, she would have to move soon.

She rose wearily to her feet, glancing about. Once again she strained her ears, but could hear nothing except the birds and the whistle of the wind through the trees. She took a step forward, then barely suppressed a shriek as a pheasant suddenly rose out of the grass just in front of her with a squawk and a rustle of wings. She watched as it struggled up and knew that the men, if they were in earshot, would almost certainly hear the bird and would guess how it had been disturbed. Now, more than ever, she had to move fast.

She glanced down at herself. The cotton blouse she wore was tight against the swell of her breasts, perspiration making it cling to her. She wished she had worn trousers, as her brown legs were scratched below her short skirt. That too clung tightly to her, showing off her beautifully rounded buttocks to perfection. She had felt good when setting out, aware of how sexy she looked, but now she felt very vulnerable indeed.

She hurried on, constantly glancing behind her and listening hard for the sound of pursuers. Although disorientated, she felt she was going the right way, but what hadn't occurred to her was that they might possibly be ahead of her, and that was her big mistake.

By the time she found herself suddenly confronted by the burly figure of one of the hunters it was too late, and she gave a cry of dismay as she realised she'd made a dreadful tactical error.

Belita's instinctive reaction was to run. She swung round, only to find herself staring into the mocking faces of two more of the men. They were relaxed now, confident of their prey, content to grin at the expression of fear so clear in Belita's young eyes.

The girl stared round from face to face, her heart thumping. They were big men, tall and broad-shouldered, and she could detect no suggestion of mercy in their expressions as they surrounded her. For a second she considered making another dash for it, but one of the men seemed to anticipate the thought and shook his head.

'There is nowhere to run, little trespasser,' he growled. 'You must face up to the consequences of invading our territory.'

Belita gazed into his eyes. He was easily the tallest of the three, and with the lean frame of one who had hunted all his life. She could never hope to outrun such a man in this environment, and her shoulders slumped as the fight left her. There was no point in trying to flee any more, she knew. They were three fit and athletic men who were intimately acquainted with the forest, while she was a lone girl, lost and far from her village.

'Wh-what do you want of me?' she asked in a tremulous voice.

'Why were you in our forest?' said the tallest.

'I-I didn't know it was your forest,' she pleaded feebly. 'I was just walking through.'

'You're lying,' accused another, a shorter man with greasy dark hair and the cruellest eyes Belita had ever seen. 'You were here to steal our goods.'

'Or to spy on us,' said the third. He was older than the other two, with streaks of grey about his temples and a weatherworn face.

'No,' she protested. 'I was just taking a shortcut.'

Moving with alarming speed, the shorter man grabbed her by the hair and wrenched her face up to his. 'Lying bitch!' he hissed. 'You're a lying bitch, and we'll show you how we treat lying bitches!'

'Stop,' she pleaded, 'you're hurting me!'

'That's the idea, peasant whore,' snarled the man. 'And we'll hurt you a whole lot more before we're through.'

Belita stared at him fearfully as he pulled her face close to his. She had known from the start that she had little hope of mercy, but the expression in his eyes told her there was no hope at all.

One of the men grasped her arms from behind, pinning her elbows together and causing her breasts to thrust forward. The men glanced at one another and sniggered as they saw how visible her smooth flesh was through the dampness of her blouse. The tall one reached out and mauled the firm outline of her soft breasts, squeezing them in his palm and sending an unexpected thrill of pleasure through her.

'Look at her nipples,' he sneered. 'The bitch likes it.'

Belita lowered her eyes, and her cheeks glowed with shame as she saw the outline of the treacherous little buds clearly pressing against the straining material, and then she inhaled sharply as another of the men rudely caressed her thrusting breasts.

The tall man said something to one of his shorter companions, who produced a length of rough rope from his knapsack and, almost before Belita knew what was happening, wound it tightly around her wrist. She tried to resist but the tall man held her fast, and then she was backed up to an overhanging tree.

Belita struggled, protesting vehemently at her rough treatment, but the ruffians ignored her cries and the tallest had no trouble tossing the rope over a branch and wrenching her arm up above her head as he made it fast. Then her other wrist was grabbed, bound and hauled up, leaving her straining on tiptoe with both hands held high above her head.

Meanwhile the older man hadn't been idle. He had pulled two stakes from his rucksack and hammered them into the ground on either side of where the hapless girl was hanging, and she begged for mercy as more rope was wrapped tightly about her ankles.

Heedless of her pitiful cries, the men pulled her legs apart and fastened them to the stakes, leaving her stretched in a taut X, the coarse ropes biting painfully into her wrists and ankles.

Once she was secure the three men stood back to admire their captive. Belita stared at them with wide eyes. Her transition to complete helplessness had been almost too sudden for her to take in, but now she knew she was totally at their mercy, and she was gripped with fear.

'That's got the slut trussed up,' grinned the short man. 'Now let's take a better

4

look at what she's hiding.'

He stepped forward and grasped Belita's blouse in grimy fists. For a second she didn't understand what was happening, then her eyes widened fearfully.

'No!' she shrieked. 'Not that, please!'

But already the man was yanking at the fragile garment, the buttons flying in all directions as he ripped it open, exposing the creamy flesh of her breasts to his lecherous stare and his companions.

Belita closed her eyes in shame as the men studied her beauty. Her firm breasts were perfectly rounded, her stiff nipples quivering deliciously as she struggled in her bonds. The man released his hold on her tattered blouse, leaving it hanging open as he grasped one erect nipple and cruelly squeezed it between finger and thumb. Belita gave a cry of pain, the tears welling in her eyes at the dreadful abuse.

And yet, even as he released her she felt something else happen to her young body; an inexplicable shiver of excitement had run down her spine at his vile touch. She fought the feeling; what these men were doing to her was wrong, and she shuddered as she thought of what might happen next.

Her captor gripped the torn material of her blouse again. One brutal tug and it ripped completely apart, reduced to a handful of useless rags, leaving her naked from the waist up, her breasts rising and falling as she tried to retain her calm. The men savoured the sight, and again exchanged knowing glances.

Belita gave a hopeless whimper as her skirt met the same fate as her top, simply ripped apart and flung aside by the hunter, and her cheeks glowed red as she hung there, clad only in tiny black panties.

'Very nice,' mumbled the older man. 'Very nice indeed.'

'Let's get a look at the rest of her,' said the tall man. 'Come on, show us the lot.'

'Please,' Belita said quietly. 'Please leave my panties on, at least.'

The short brute guffawed. 'You should've thought about your modesty before you trespassed in our forest, you slut,' he spat. 'Strip her.'

The brief panties were snatched from Belita in a single swift movement. She stared at the useless piece of black lace that had been her last concession to modesty, now lying discarded in the grass. Then her eyes dropped to her own pale body. Through the valley between her breasts she could see the dark mound of her pubis. She knew that, with her legs spread as they were, the pinkness of her sex was exposed for the gawping ruffians. She had never felt so naked, stretched taut, unable to meet their hungry bloodshot eyes as they passed lewd and suggestive comments about her.

Then the short man moved closer to her, laying a hairy hand flat on her belly. She tried to pull away, but there was nothing she could do to stop him as it slid possessively down towards the soft downy hairs between her thighs.

'Please, no...' she whispered feebly as stubby fingers found the little bud of her clitoris, bringing a shameful spasm of extraordinary pleasure such as she had never experienced before. She was quite unable to reconcile her emotions as she hung there in bondage. On the one hand there was fear and shame at the helplessness of her situation, yet somehow the coarse fingers were doing something to her that she had never dreamed possible. They were bringing her pleasure such as she had never experienced before, and she could not suppress a quiet groan of delight as he toyed with her.

A finger pushed up into her vagina, and the man grinned as he heard her groan again and felt her wet warmth clutching his intrusive digit. 'The little slut is hot for it,' he said.

'All in good time,' said the older one. 'We'll give her what she wants, but first she must discover how we punish young women who trespass on our land.'

As he spoke he began pulling the belt from his trousers, and Belita watched in horrified fascination. She waited for him to undo the button at his waist, but instead he doubled the thick leather in his fist, looked into her eyes, then with a sudden movement he brought the belt down hard against his palm, the crack making her jump fearfully and echoing through the trees.

The short man eased his finger deeper into her sex, and then pulled it out, eliciting a gasp from the helpless beauty. He held up his hand and Belita blushed anew as they all gazed upon the juices that coated it, and then he wiped it across her belly, leaving glistening streaks on her pale flesh. Then he nodded to the man with the belt.

'Six strokes each, I think,' he said. 'Then we'll show her the prowess of men from the forest.'

The tall man giggled insanely. 'My cock's already straining to get into this little beauty,' he said.

'I want to feel those pretty lips about my shaft,' said the older man. 'Now stand aside, let's add some colour to that cute little backside.'

The other two stood back, and Belita watched fearfully as he swept the belt through the air two more times.

'Please,' she pleaded. 'I'll do whatever you ask.'

'Certainly you will,' he said. 'Once you've been punished.'

He drew back the belt, and Belita closed her eyes as she heard it descend.

Swish! *Whack*!

The cruel leather bit into the soft flesh of her bottom. For a moment she felt nothing, then the dreadful pain coursed through her and she screamed.

Swish! *Whack*!

He wasted no time in bringing the belt down again, placing another vicious welt across her unprotected buttocks as the broad band bit into her. This time the pain was even worse than before, and sparkling tears began to flow down her cheeks.

Swish! *Whack*!
Swish! *Whack*!

He was beating her with all his strength, her naked body rocking forward in its tight bondage as the belt cracked against her vulnerable backside. The pain seemed unbearable now, yet still he relentlessly beat her.

Swish! *Whack*!
Swish! *Whack*!

Then the beating stopped for a moment, the sobbing girl shaking as the agony coursed through her. She strained to glance over her shoulder, her tearstained eyes barely able to discern what was happening. Then she gave a cry of despair as she realised he had passed his belt to the tall man, who was taking practice swings with it.

The older brute moved in front of her and she closed her eyes in shame as she felt her soft breasts being mauled. He took his time, ignoring her whispered pleas for mercy, running his hands over her nubile body, and then she gasped as once again a long thick finger penetrated her vagina.

She moaned softly, the fire in her behind momentarily forgotten as her sex muscles contracted about his digit. Then she blinked aside her tears and the moan turned to one of despair as her vision cleared. The man had undone his breeches, and protruding from them was a gnarled, erect penis. He was stroking it pensively while licking his brown teeth.

'Yeah, slut,' he grinned. 'This is what's coming to you.'

Then he withdrew his finger, and Belita heard the belt come swiping down once more.

Chapter 2

Somewhere nearby bells were ringing, their incessant rise and fall like someone practising scales in ever-changing tempo. The sound wormed its way into Laura's consciousness, slowly bringing her out of her reverie. She shook her head as she suddenly realised where she was. As she did so, something slipped from her lap onto the grass. Still not fully awake she reached down for the object. It was a book, bound in leather and quite old. As she picked it up it fell open to an illustration, showing a naked girl tied to a tree, her buttocks striped with welts.

Laura felt the colour rise in her cheeks as she remembered the chapter she had just read, the story of the peasant girl captured and whipped by the hunters. It was, she told herself, a dreadful story. How could anyone write such a thing? What on earth had made her read it?

Yet, deep inside, she knew what had motivated her. Somehow she had found the story extraordinarily exciting - stimulating in a way she had never imagined words on paper could be.

Then, staring again at the disturbing picture, she knew she'd been dreaming it was her, not the fictional Belita, who was at the mercy of the hunters, and that she too could feel the heat and wetness between her legs so graphically described in the tale.

She snapped the book shut, suddenly feeling unaccountably guilty about her reaction to it. She glanced at the spine. *The Enslavement of Belita* did not exactly mark it out as classical literature. Yet, when she had found the hidden cabinet in her guardian's library that afternoon, and saw the array of unusual tomes therein, this had been the book her hands had strayed to.

The chimes penetrated her consciousness once more and she glanced towards the church tower from which they came. As she did so she spotted the time on its clock.

It was nearly seven o'clock, so she sighed and rose to her feet. The sun's rays were still warm on this balmy summer evening, but she could tarry no longer in the garden. Dinner was at seven-thirty sharp, and she was always expected to be on time. Reluctantly she made her way up the garden towards the forbidding pile that was her guardian's house.

It was a large garden, larger than most people even dream of having. Surrounded by a high red brick wall it stretched more than two hundred yards down to a small lake, where a number of waterfowl were swimming. On the far side was a thick copse of trees, with a pathway winding through. These were mature trees that testified to the age of the garden, and their twisted branches reached up for the sky, laden with lush green leaves. Nearer the house the garden was laid out with flowerbeds, each one a riot of bright summer colours, with trellises festooned with climbing plants.

To many the run of such a garden would have been an unimaginable luxury, with its twisting pathways, sweet-smelling blooms and great expanses of lawns. To Laura Spender, however, the garden was more like a prison than a paradise, where she sat day after day on the bench by the lake, staring across at the high walls and imagining what was happening beyond them.

It seemed an age to Laura since she had last been allowed to leave the confines of the house to wander freely beyond. She yearned to do just that, maybe to go out with other girls of her own age.

These days her only escape was her guardian's books, and she had been working her way through his collection for some time, voraciously devouring title after title.

It was only that morning that she had discovered the secret cabinet, though. The books in there were very different from those on display on the other shelves. At first she had closed the door and turned away, but something about the titles caught her imagination, and she returned. Quite why she chose *The Enslavement of Belita* she wasn't sure. All she knew was that once she started the story, she became totally engrossed in it.

Laura had been living in the house for more than a year, ever since her parents were killed in an air crash and Sir John Carworth had become her guardian. Sir John, as her father's closest living relative, had been executor of the will and named as the one to take charge of her needs. At the age of majority, as defined by the will, her father's legacy would pass to her. It was no small sum, and Laura was destined to become comfortably rich once she received it. However, that day was two years away and, until it came, she was under the control of Sir John, and obliged to live as he decreed.

And he decreed that she live the life of a hermit. Sir John was a financier, a public figure and a friend of the government. Scarcely a week passed when he wasn't featured in some prominent news story in the papers or on television. He had explained to his young ward that this made her vulnerable, both to entrapment by the press and to the danger of kidnap. Although she had insisted that since nobody knew who she was she was relatively safe outside the confines of the house, he would have none of it, and she was seldom allowed out without a chaperone and a large limousine to carry her.

Laura let herself in by a side door that led into the servants' quarters. Her guardian was entertaining some important guests and she didn't fancy having to go through the formalities of introductions. She crept down the bare corridor past the laundry room, then up a back staircase that led to the landing near her bedroom, and she slipped inside and closed the door, thankful to have encountered nobody.

She just had time for a shower before being called to eat, so unbuttoning her white blouse she shrugged it off, slipped off her shoes, peeled her jeans down and then, dressed only in bra and panties, went into her bathroom and ran the shower to the temperature she wanted.

She slipped out of her skimpy underwear, and then stepped beneath the steaming water. It felt so good, as if washing away the cares of the day, and she lingered, enjoying the refreshing sensation.

Emerging from the shower her pale skin glistened with droplets of water. She reached for one of the heavy white towels that hung beside the bath and wrapped it about herself, hugging it to her cool skin and allowing it to absorb the moisture. Then she wandered through into her bedroom to pick out a dress for dinner.

There was a full-length mirror in the bedroom and she paused in front of it, examining her features. Laura was beautiful by any standards; she had well-defined cheekbones and large green eyes that had an innocence to them that would have softened the hardest of hearts. Her nose was like an elegant sculpture, her mouth small, but with full lips that seemed pursed ready to be kissed. Her face was framed by long auburn hair that hung down below her shoulders.

On a sudden whim Laura let the towel slip from her body and fall to the floor in a damp heap. She allowed her eyes to travel down her body, her expression critical, though despite being a modest girl it would have been very difficult to find fault with what she saw. Laura's breasts were round and firm, and the coolness of the water had caused her nipples to stiffen, and they stood proudly, surrounded by the crimped areolae. There was absolutely no hint of sag to her breasts, making the brassiere she had discarded somewhat superfluous.

Her torso tapered down to a slim waist, with a flat stomach punctuated by a neat navel. Her hips were full but not wide, and her delicate dark thatch of pubic hair scarcely covered the lips of her sex.

She turned and, glancing over her shoulder, examined the pale flawless skin of her back and the soft swell of her beautifully rounded bottom. Her eyes dropped lower still, following the contours of her shapely legs down to her neat ankles and dainty feet.

Laura had an idea that she was attractive, but her separation from young men and women of her own age meant that she had never quite understood how exquisite she really was. Now, as she took in her image she thought of Belita, and of the illustrations. Almost without thinking she widened her stance and raised her hands above her head in imitation of the picture of the girl in the book. She noted how her breasts stretched into a firm oval, and the way the lips of her sex parted as she took up the stance. She thought of the beating and imagined the sensation of the belt cracking across her behind, and as she thought of it she almost subconsciously let her hand drift down to her pubis, ran her fingers through the wispy down, then began gently teasing the prominent bud of her sex. She had played with herself before, and she found herself shivering, as she always did, at the strange sensations she experienced. This time, though, the sensations were stronger than ever. Something about what she'd been reading had made her wetter and more sensitive than ever, and now as she rubbed herself she felt a sense of excitement building inside her such as she had never known.

The sound of the dinner gong, far below in the house, shook the beauty from her reverie and she snatched her fingers away, her cheeks glowing with shame. She glanced around, afraid she might have been seen, then realised she had to get a move on or she might be late for dinner and incur the wrath of her guardian.

Snatching a pair of panties and a bra from a drawer she put them on, pulled a dress over her head, dragged a comb quickly through her hair, slipped on her flat shoes, and made a dash for the door.

Some minutes later the door to the bedroom opened again and a woman entered. It was not Laura, but an older woman, tall and slender with her dark hair tied up in a bun. She wore a plain black dress that clung tightly to her curves, and she had a proprietorial air about her as she walked about the room, tut-tutting at the discarded clothes on the floor. She picked them up, along with the towel, and then spent a minute or so tidying the bathroom.

She was about to leave when her hawkish gaze fell on the book lying on the bed, and she paused. She crossed to the bed, picked up the book and began leafing through the pages. There was a bookmark at the illustration showing the naked girl receiving her punishment, and the woman stared at the picture, and then cast her eyes over the writing. She spent a few more silent minutes examining the text, then closed the book and stared at the cover, a thoughtful look on her face.

Chapter 3

Laura lay on her bed, eyes glued to the pages of the book, regularly turning the pages as she devoured every word of the lurid story. The hapless Belita, long since deprived of her virginity by the rough band of hunters, had been enslaved by the people of the forest and was now the subject of regular beatings and humiliation.

As Laura read on the peasant girl found herself tied kneeling to a whipping post in the centre of the forest people's encampment. One by one the men queued up to thrust their stiff cocks into the naked captive's mouth, spilling their seed down her throat while behind her a muscular brute stood with a whip, lashing her pale flesh whenever she showed signs of flagging.

Laura was quite unable to comprehend her fascination with Belita's story as it unfolded on the pages before her. Normally she found refuge from her dull existence in romances by classical authors, and never before had she encountered such a tale of cruelty and uncontrolled lust. Yet it wasn't simply the tale of a helpless victim and her captors that held her attention. Time after time Laura read descriptions of the most extraordinary orgasms enjoyed by the girl as one or other of her masters took his pleasure in her lovely body and, as each new indignity was heaped upon the young slave, so her own passions grew.

It was this aspect, the sheer eroticism of the story, that was holding Laura's attention. She, like Belita at the beginning of the book, was a virgin with virtually no experience of sexual encounters. The convent school to which her parents sent her had not allowed any mention of sex, either in the classrooms or in the dormitories. Even private nudity was banned, with the girls putting on and removing their clothes under the cover of the diaphanous nightgowns the nuns forced them to wear in bed. In the showers and bathrooms they were strictly segregated, and had been taught that to touch themselves was sinful. Now, as she read the story of lust and degradation, Laura found it difficult to reconcile her inner feelings with the way she had been taught.

What she did know was that the story was having a physical effect on her. Beneath her light cotton nightshirt she could see the way her nipples had stiffened to hard points, just as Belita's did when the men caressed her breasts or beat them with their whips. Between her legs even stranger things were happening. The more she read about Belita's experiences the more Laura found her own sex reacting in the same way as the peasant girl's. An odd warmth and wetness was invading her, threatening to leak from the very portals of her most private place. On more than one occasion she slipped a hand down and was astounded at the way her muscles convulsed as she touched the hard bud of her clitoris.

Laura was in turmoil. On the one hand she knew that touching between her legs induced the most extraordinary sensations of pleasure, in the same way it did to Belita when the men molested her. Yet such pleasure was wrong, she told herself whilst finding it virtually impossible to put down the book, each new violation of its young heroine bringing fresh spasms of pleasure to her.

She turned the page, and gave a little gasp as she saw the illustration there. It showed Belita completely naked, spreadeagled across a table in the middle of the forest people's camp. Her wrists and ankles were secured to the corners of the table and her sex was exposed. The men had shaved her crotch, and Laura found herself staring at her vagina, drawn as it was in loving detail by the artist. She studied the erect bud of Belita's clitoris, and at the glistening moisture that seeped from her. Her eyes travelled up to the captive's belly and breasts. They were streaked with the marks of the whip, which was even now descending onto her helpless body. But what most held Laura's attention was the man who stood between Belita's open legs, his breeches discarded, his cock standing erect as he stroked the swollen helmet, his eyes fixed on the girl's sex.

Laura closed the book, suddenly overcome with guilt at her fascination. She stretched out on the bed, her heart pounding, her mind filled with the image. She lay like that for many minutes, her eyes tightly closed. There was a desire inside her that she had never encountered before and, try as she might, she couldn't rid her mind of it. Then, unable to fight her desires any longer, she opened the book again and sat up.

She laid the book beside her on the duvet and hesitantly reached for the hem of her nightgown. Opposite her was the mirror, and she glanced at the reflection, blushing slightly as she caught sight of her face. Then, slowly, she began to raise the garment, pulling it up her thighs until the dark patch of her pubic hair was revealed. She paused for a moment, holding her breath, and then with a decisive movement she dragged it up over her head and dropped it to the floor.

She glanced down at her nakedness, the remonstrations of the nuns returned, but then she gazed at the illustration again and the nuns were forgotten. She studied the position of the girl, her eyes taking in every inch of her body. Then she lay back and stretched her arms out to the corners of the bed, at the same time widening her legs so that she took up a pose exactly like that of Belita. She raised her head and stared at her pale form; her firm breasts stood proudly from her chest, the nipples like hard buds. Her eyes travelled lower to the prominent mound of her pubis, below which she knew her slit was open, revealing the wetness within, and she wished she could see it.

Perhaps...

Laura rose and crossed to the dressing table, opened a drawer and pulled out a vanity mirror on a stand. Then she climbed back onto the bed, took another glance at the illustration, then placed the mirror between her legs and adopted the spreadeagled pose once more.

She lay for a few seconds more, then raised her head and glanced down between her breasts. A shiver ran through her as she caught sight of her open sex, the lips parted so that the shiny wetness was visible. She stared at her clitoris; an inflamed pink bud glistening with moisture.

She remained as she was for a number of minutes, occasionally glancing at the picture beside her. She found her eyes drawn to the erection of the man, whose view between the peasant girl's legs was almost identical to that between her own. She found herself riveted by the thought of what was about to happen to Belita, so she picked up the book once more and began to read on.

The story told how the girl was forced to watch helplessly as the man climbed between her open thighs, his stiff cock still in his fist. As he slumped over her she struggled with the bonds, but in vain. The leering brute simply guided his gnarled cock between her nether lips and lunged, possessing her with a single thrust.

As she read the account of Belita's violation, Laura felt the muscles of her own sex twitch, and pushed her bottom up from the duvet as if it was she, not Belita, who was being impaled by that monstrous cock.

Laura's free hand seemed to make its own way down between her thighs. One minute it was resting above her head as if tied to the bedpost, and the next her fingertips found her clitoris.

She gave a sharp intake of breath as she began to rub gently. At once a delicious sensation filled her and she moaned softly, pressing up against her hand, rubbing harder as she felt an urgency rising within her.

Through misty eyes she read on, slipping two fingers into her vagina and pumping them urgently, her imagination transforming the fingers into the penis of the ogre taking his pleasure in Belita.

'Well, well, that stuff really gets you going, doesn't it?'

Laura gave a stifled scream at the sound of the voice, dropping the book as if it were red hot and clamping a hand across her vagina as she crossed her legs and covered her breasts with her other hand.

'Wh-what...?'

'Don't cover yourself up on my account, Laura. I was enjoying that.'

The housekeeper, in her usual black, smiled a cold smile, looking down imperiously at the mortified girl doing her best to hide her nakedness as she crimsoned with shame.

'Wh-what do you want, C-Cassandra?' stammered Laura.

'I just came to see how much you're enjoying the book,' she answered, her voice devoid of warmth. 'And by the look of it, the answer is very much.'

Poor Laura just wanted the duvet to swallow her up. She couldn't believe such a thing was happening. 'But - but why...?' she blurted.

'Well, I saw it on the bed when I tidied your room earlier.'

'But...'

'And I know it's from Sir John's secret collection,' she went on, contemptuously ignoring Laura's feeble protestations.

Laura sudden felt very sick and very small. 'You... you won't tell him, will you?' she said weakly.

'Why should I?' the woman said airily. 'After all, you're his ward, and I'm just one of the servants.' She gracefully settled her neat bottom on the bed beside

Laura, as though comforting an ailing child. 'So,' she went on dispassionately, compounding Laura's shame by not mentioning her nakedness or the disgraceful act she'd been caught indulging in, 'what's the book about?'

Laura felt her cheeks glowing even more. 'Nuh-nothing,' she muttered, but was too late to stop the woman as she snatched it up, still open at the page Laura had been masturbating over.

'Somewhat kinky,' she commented. 'I knew Sir John was into this type of thing, but I never suspected it of you too.'

Laura was feeling terrible. 'I... I was just interested, that's all,' she said sulkily.

'Just interested, eh?' the austere woman scoffed. 'And tell me, Laura, how often do you lie on your bed naked and masturbate?'

Laura was astounded by the suggestion. 'I-I've never done it before,' she said indignantly.

'I don't believe you.'

'It's true I tell you. It was just, well, it was that book. I've never read anything like that before.'

'And the bondage and CP turned you on?'

'Wh-what's CP?'

'Corporal punishment; whipping, caning and such like,' the woman explained with the air of a patient schoolteacher. 'You find that a turn on?'

'No...' Laura denied, 'I mean, I don't know. Please leave me alone now.'

'What, with you in such a state?' the woman countered with an elaborate frown of concern. 'That wouldn't be very fair, now would it? Why don't I help you relieve all that tension first?'

Laura stared at her. 'What... what do you mean?' she asked carefully.

'Only that I happen to have something here that you'll find much more fun than your fingers.'

So flustered had Laura been upon being discovered, that she only now noticed for the first time that the woman was carrying a velvet bag, and watched as manicured fingers began undoing the cord that held it closed. They dipped effortlessly inside and pulled something out, and as Laura saw it clearly for the first time, she clamped her hands to her mouth and gasped with shock.

It was an artificial penis, perfect in every alarming detail. Laura had never seen a real one, in the flesh, but she knew this was a very realistic model. But what shocked her more than anything was the size; at least ten inches long, and wide about the girth. She shivered at the sight of it.

'It's a beauty, isn't it?' said Cassandra, a hint of emotion creeping into her voice for the first time. 'Here, take it.'

She held it out but Laura drew back. 'No,' she said. 'Please leave me alone, Cassandra.'

'So you can get on with masturbating in private?' the woman said scornfully, increasing the girl's shame. 'Come on Laura, you can tell me; what is it about the book that's turned you on so?'

'It... it's none of it.'

'Oh, come now.' Cassandra flipped the page to another illustration. Belita was tied supine over a barrel, one man thrusting into her sex while another fucked her mouth, with yet more waiting their turn. 'There now,' said Cassandra, showing the picture to Laura. 'Don't you wish that was you tied at their mercy?'

Laura lowered her eyes and said nothing, as Cassandra gently stroked her hair. 'Have you never had an orgasm?' she asked softly.

Laura hesitated, and then shook her head.

'But you're feeling aroused now.' She reached down and pushed Laura's protective hand away from between her thighs. Laura offered a futile attempt to clench them together to keep the intruding fingers at bay, but Cassandra was not to be denied.

She eased her fingers into Laura's sex, making the girl gasp and shudder, and when she lifted them away they were coated with a sheen of moisture. 'You see?' she purred. 'That wetness tells me everything. Now lie like you were, as if you were tied to the bed.'

'No...' said Laura. 'Please leave me alone.'

'Come on, Laura. You wouldn't want me to tell Sir John you've been raiding his secret book collection, would you?'

'You wouldn't... would you?' the girl asked timidly.

'I will if you don't co-operate.' She smiled thinly. 'Now, no more petulance, young lady, or I might have to tell about your disgusting little secret.'

Laura looked at the woman. There was no doubt she was serious. Yet how could she possibly submit to her demands? Then she thought of Belita, and how that girl's submissiveness had been such a turn on, and a small shiver of excitement ran through her. Surely the situation couldn't be arousing her? Yet, as she thought of the peasant girl forced to submit to the vile forest people, she experienced another pulse of anticipation. She looked at the woman beside her, recognising in her eyes the amusement and the cruelty of Belita's captors, and suddenly knew she wanted to submit - to lose herself again in the fantasy of the book.

Slowly, reluctantly, she moved her arm from across her breasts, revealing her succulent orbs to the older woman. Her cheeks glowing, she reached up to the corners of the bed, grasping hold of the wooden posts. Then she let her thighs part, sliding her ankles to the lower corners. 'Like this?' she asked timidly.

The woman nodded. 'That's better,' she said. 'Now remember, your wrists and ankles are tied. You can't move. Understand?'

'Yes, I understand.' The words sent another delicious tremor through Laura's naked body. She was Belita now, tied and helpless before her uncaring captor, her body for the taking, and when Cassandra reached out and cupped a marble-cold hand over her breast she gave a start, but kept her grip firmly on the stout bedposts.

'What pretty breasts,' Cassandra cooed, squeezing the soft flesh possessively and running her fingers over the engorged nipples. 'Has a man ever laid a hand on these, Laura?'

'No,' she whispered, trying hard to keep her voice steady. Having her breasts touched was an extraordinary sensation, and it was all she could do to prevent herself moaning her approval.

'Such soft skin,' murmured the housekeeper. 'And so yielding to the touch. But of course you're yielding. You're my captive, aren't you?'

Laura nodded.

'And you're helpless to stop me, aren't you?'

'Yes,' she said. 'I'm helpless. I'm your captive.'

As Laura spoke the words the woman squeezed her breasts tighter, pinching the nipples between finger and thumb. 'See how your teats swell,' she murmured. 'That shows how turned on you are, Laura. Look at them, standing up like little cherries.'

Laura glanced down at her breasts. Her nipples were indeed erect, and her pulse raced as the woman stroked them.

'Now, Laura,' the housekeeper went on, 'you remember the way the girl in the book gets fucked? Well, I want you to imagine that man lying over you, poised over your frail nudity. You can smell his foul sweat, Laura, and the stench of stale alcohol on his breath. You can feel his hard cock brushing against your belly, and you're powerless to stop it.'

As she spoke she picked up the phallus and began touching her captive with it. Laura flinched as she felt the artificial helmet against her tingling flesh, but she remained still, pinned to the bed by the authority of the woman.

Cassandra moved the thing lower, and it began to vibrate with a low buzzing sound. Laura nibbled her lip as she felt it slide down over her pubic mound.

'*Ah...*' Her entire body convulsed as the vibrator sought her clitoris. Laura had never imagined such a sensation, and her sensitive bud suddenly sent a spasm of exquisite delight coursing through her body.

Cassandra smiled. 'Good,' she said. 'I see you're ready for it. Ready to be forcibly taken by this coarse stranger. You want that, don't you Laura? You want to give yourself to him.'

'Y-yes,' gasped the girl. 'Please, do it now.'

The woman moved the throbbing vibrator lower, sliding it back and forth across Laura's sex lips, which glistened with moisture. The girl shuddered at the intimacy of the touch, and found herself anxious to feel the thick cock deep inside her yearning vagina.

And as the desire overwhelmed her Cassandra pressed against the pink petals of her sex, twisting the phallus slightly as she drove it between Laura's open thighs. The supine beauty gave a dreamy cry as she felt the bulbous glans penetrate her, invading her sex as Cassandra continued to feed it ever deeper, until its entire length was buried inside her.

Cassandra paused then, staring with no evident emotion at the writhing girl on the bed; eyes tightly shut, jaw clenched, thigh muscles spasming, her beautiful breasts quivering as she breathed deeply.

With carefully calculated method Cassandra began moving the phallus back and forth, bringing fresh cries from the girl. Laura was lost, her mind filled with the fantasy of being Belita, strapped to a rough table, her legs spread for the uncaring stranger whilst others waited their turn. She imagined the vibrating obscenity to be a living cock, violating her, bringing her pleasure such as she had never imagined. Her passions increased, her head rolling from side to side as a series of whimpered screams escaped her lips.

Faster still the dildo pumped. Laura panted, her breasts rising and falling with a staccato movement as her orgasm approached. Her hands were balled into fists and her eyes were screwed tight as she felt herself reaching her peak.

She came with a cry, her imaginary bonds forgotten as she thrust her pubis up against Cassandra's hand, forcing the thick vibrator still deeper into her as she savoured the extraordinary pleasure of her orgasm. All pretence of modesty was forgotten as she extracted every last ounce of joy from the buzzing, alien monstrosity.

At last she could take no more, and only then did she relax, lowering her bottom to the bed once more, her cries turning to replete sighs. Cassandra slowed her hand, letting the girl come down gently, until finally she was still save for the gentle rising and falling of her delicious breasts as her breathing calmed.

Cassandra sat quietly, gazing down as the girl opened her eyes, her cheeks glowing with shame.

'Yes, Laura,' she said. 'I'm going to enjoy training you in the arts of pleasure.'

Chapter 4

Cassandra opened the top drawer on her dresser and dropped the velvet bag into it. She smiled slightly as she pushed the drawer shut and turned the tiny key in the lock. Who would have thought the girl would be turned on by her guardian's collection of erotica? That had been an unexpected bonus, and one she knew she could exploit to the utmost.

She left her quarters and made her way silently along the landing. The house was silent, the master and his wife having long since retired to bed and the rest of the servants to their own part of the house. She knew she would not be disturbed as she let herself into the library and closed the door silently behind her.

Cassandra turned on the light and glanced about. The walls of the room were lined with books, many of them very old. On the far side was the reference section, with row upon row of large tomes. It was towards these shelves full of dictionaries and encyclopaedias that the housekeeper made her way, though it was neither a dictionary nor an encyclopaedia she was seeking. Instead, she dropped to her knees and reached for a small, unobtrusive knob in the woodwork. A panel slid open, revealing more bookshelves within.

She wondered idly how Laura had come to find the secret hidey-hole, but the whys and wherefores were not particularly important.

Unlike the reference books there was no uniformity to this part of the library. It was a mixture of books, some old and well worn, others more modern. Many were paperbacks with alluring pictures of scantily clad beauties on the covers.

Cassandra began leafing through the volumes with purpose. She was seeking something similar to the book she had found in Laura's possession; something that would have the desired effect on Sir John's young ward. Having searched through a few of the paperbacks her attention moved to another shelf of larger books with soft covers. She slid them out and found the volume she wanted, a faint smile crossing her lips.

It was an illustrated copy of *The Story of O*; precisely what she needed to further ensnare the mouth-watering girl; to lure her into her web.

Cassandra closed the cupboard carefully and headed back to her quarters.

Back in the shadows of her semi-dark room Cassandra stripped off her clothes, taking the opportunity to run her hands adoringly over her own full breasts. Although Cassandra was tall and slender, they were heavier than Laura's, but still firm with large nipples. She eyed them with pride, aware that their beauty would arouse any red-blooded male.

Her panties whispered over her bottom and down her legs, revealing a thick bush of jet-black pubic hair, and her hips swayed as she made her way to the bathroom. She turned on the taps and the steam began to rise as the bath filled, and soon she was lying back allowing the hot soapy water to ease and relax the day's aches and pains away.

She thought about the girl, and a calculating smile of satisfaction crossed her face. She had been looking for a way to get back at Sir John Carworth, but had not expected the means to fall so easily into her grasp.

Cassandra Kurwen had not always hated Sir John. When he had first employed her, more than ten years before, she was happy to work in the house and took to the job with enthusiasm. In those days, though, her father was butler, and managed the servants with a strict but benign regime that most were happy to work under. Cassandra started as a maid, but was soon taking on more responsibilities, as her talents became known to her employers.

For nearly seven years the status quo had been maintained. Then came the incident of the theft.

It happened one evening; Sir John was entertaining a number of important guests. Everything had gone well until they were leaving. Cassandra had been supervising the distribution of the guests' coats when one of them complained that his wallet was missing from his coat pocket.

In the ensuing row the wallet was found with its contents removed, outside the door to the butler's room. The guest ordered the room be searched, and they found money and credit cards stashed in a drawer. From the start her father protested his innocence, claiming he had left his door unlocked and that anyone could have planted the wallet's contents. Another maid came forward and admitted seeing an ex-employee hanging about the house that afternoon; a man her father had sacked a few weeks earlier for dishonesty, and Cassandra was convinced from the start that this was the real culprit.

But Sir John would have none of it, and following another vehement row her father was summarily dismissed and ordered to leave the house the following day. Cassandra, disgusted with his treatment, was determined to leave with him and packed her bags, but he persuaded her to stay, pointing out that to leave might associate her with his dismissal, thus making it difficult for her to find a new position elsewhere.

Unable to find employment with such a blemish on his record her father went into rapid decline, drinking too much and becoming more and more depressed. Eventually, in a drunken stupor, he fell from a bus and was run over and killed, and from that day Cassandra vowed to take revenge on Sir John and his family.

At first her plans were simple ones. Set fire to the house, save her wages to hire a hit man, or sabotage one of the cars. But it soon occurred to her that such plans were too crude and would, in the end, do more harm to her than to Sir John. What she needed was some way to disgrace him in his public and political life, and now, at last, she had the catalyst she'd been searching for. It had all the right ingredients. The British tabloids were obsessed with sex and, to have a scandal involving the privileged was precisely what they would be looking for in a good story. All she had to do was manipulate the girl to get the maximum impact from the story.

She thought of the delicious creature stretched submissively on the bed, and had no doubt that if she could exploit the girl's sexual inquisitiveness, she could arrange for Sir John's downfall in a very spectacular fashion.

Cassandra stretched luxuriously in the steaming water and allowed herself a thin smile. There was no hurry. She would enjoy corrupting that lovely young creature almost as much as she would enjoy the downfall of her guardian.

Chapter 5

Laura lay on her bed, turning the pages of the large illustrated book and devouring the extraordinarily erotic images there, confused again by the shameful way her body was responding to them.

She had discovered the book lying on her pillow when she returned from lunch, and knew at once that she would find its contents fascinating, just as she had the others. Somehow she didn't seem able to resist the allure of the books, and this one held her attention right from the very first page.

It was more than two weeks since her strange encounter with the housekeeper, and since then a steady stream of erotic, sado-masochistic literature had been arriving in her room. Each book was more outrageous than the last, and she was amazed that such literature could exist. Yet her fascination with it was undiminished.

She knew Cassandra was supplying the books, and she knew too that she should resist the temptation to read them. Indeed, when *The Story of O* appeared she refused to open it for two days, hiding it away in her dresser, but every time she returned to her room it would be laying on her pillow, it's lurid cover illustration challenging her to open it. At last she succumbed and devoured the book with relish, masturbating feverishly as her senses were overwhelmed by what she saw and read.

Apart from covertly delivering the literature, Cassandra had not bothered her since that fateful evening. Laura was left alone to pursue her fantasies and she was grateful for that, although she often thought hungrily of that monstrous vibrator. She used her fingers, but they were no substitute for that wonderful column of buzzing plastic.

The sound of the door opening dragged Laura back to her senses. She slammed the book shut and swung round, her face red with guilt, as there stood Cassandra. She was dressed, as always, in plain black, and she held a small velvet bag. For a moment Laura's pulse skipped, but she knew the bag was too small to contain the tormentor she'd just been wistfully contemplating.

'Don't you ever knock?' she asked, mustering what dignity she could in her flustered state.

'Are you enjoying the book, Laura?' asked the housekeeper, ignoring her question.

Laura looked down at the volume on her pillow. 'I... I suppose so,' she said sullenly. 'It's like all the others, really.'

'And does it turn you on?' the woman asked directly.

'Why are you always asking me such questions?' asked Laura. 'It's all very personal and unfair.'

'Because you have so much to learn, to offer, and to enjoy, Laura.'

'I - I do?'

Cassandra smiled and nodded. 'You do. Remember how good the vibrator felt?'

Laura pouted. 'It - it wasn't fair of you to take advantage of me like that.'

'Who was taking advantage? You loved it, didn't you? It seems to me the advantage was all yours.'

Laura was flustered by Cassandra's confident demeanour, and blurted, 'Why do you keep leaving these books in my room?'

'Because you keep enjoying them,' the housekeeper replied calmly, with infuriating logic.

Laura glanced down guiltily at the book that lay on her pillow and said nothing, and Cassandra sat on the bed beside her. Laura was wearing a short summer dress, leaving her slender legs bare, and the housekeeper ran her fingers over the smooth flesh.

'Don't you want to learn more about the pleasure your body can bring you,

Laura?'

The girl shifted uncomfortably; the book had already roused her passions before the woman invaded her privacy, and Cassandra's perfume was evoking unwelcome memories of their earlier encounter, and the cool touch on her flesh was conspiring with that scent to increase her excitement. 'What... what were you thinking of?' she asked quietly.

Cassandra picked up the book and flicked through it. She reached a page and held it up to Laura; a large illustration depicting a naked girl with her hands tied behind her back, standing before a group of natives in tribal regalia. On the page opposite was another picture in which one of the men had dropped his loincloth, his huge penis standing erect while others were pressing the girl onto her back.

'Last time we only pretended your arms were tied,' Cassandra whispered. 'This time I've got something here to do it for real.'

She reached into the bag and pulled out a length of cord, and Laura felt her stomach tighten. She glanced back at the illustrations, and then took a deep breath to calm her racing pulse.

'I... I don't think so, Cassandra,' she said, without conviction.

'You don't crave the idea?'

Laura reddened. 'Why should I?'

'Because you clearly like the pictures.'

'But, that's different,' Laura countered weakly. 'They're just pictures.'

'Indeed they are,' Cassandra agreed smoothly, 'and don't you think the real thing would be even more exciting?'

Laura fidgeted uncomfortably, feeling increasingly cornered. 'It's just not right, that's all.'

'Of course it's not right, and that's what makes it so dangerously fun. Come on, you'll always live with regret if you don't even try.'

Laura looked at the cord, and the thought of being bound with it was exciting her more than she dared admit; to the woman - or to herself. She closed her eyes for a few seconds, needing to think.

'It wouldn't hurt, would it?' she asked quietly.

'A little... it's no fun if it doesn't hurt a wee bit.'

Laura stared into the older woman's eyes. 'I mean, you'd stop if I wasn't happy, wouldn't you?'

Cassandra smiled. 'Of course I will,' she purred silkily, confidently changing the tense of the exchange.

Laura nibbled her lip, and then said, 'All right... just for a little while.'

'Good. I knew you wanted to really. Come on then.'

'What do you mean?' asked Laura anxiously. 'Where are we going?'

The woman stroked Laura's hair. 'We're going to be a little bit adventurous.'

'I - I don't understand,' Laura blurted, feeling her panic rising. 'Where are you taking me?'

'You'll see. Come on.'

Laura rose slowly to her feet, slipped on a pair of sandals, and followed the housekeeper out of the door and down the corridor, her heart drumming wildly. As they walked in silence she glanced about guiltily. Her guardian and his wife were out for the afternoon, she knew, and most of the servants would not be around at this time of day, but she felt as though she was being watched as they made their way down the empty passageway.

When Cassandra opened the back door that led out to the garden Laura paused again.

'What are you doing?' she asked.

'It's such a lovely afternoon,' Cassandra replied easily. 'I'm going outside.'

'But I thought...'

Cassandra took her hand. 'Trust me, Laura,' she said.

The girl allowed herself to be led down the path. It was indeed a beautiful day; the sun was shining brightly from a clear blue sky and felt good on her shoulders and legs. In ordinary circumstances she would have been happy to be out strolling in the garden in such weather, but these were not ordinary circumstances.

Cassandra took her down to the bottom of the garden and through an arched wooden gate in the wall. As Laura followed she glanced about in surprise; she had thought she knew the garden well, but this was somewhere she had never visited before.

The secret area was dense with vegetation, and in its shade Laura suddenly felt a little chilly. All around her were whispering trees, with a dirt path meandering between them. Above she could hear the sound of wood pigeons calling, and the sun cast dappled shadows across the grass.

Cassandra led her prey a little further to where the trees opened into a grassy area. 'There,' she said, 'isn't this just perfect?'

'It is beautiful,' Laura admitted, her eyes wide as she gazed around at the beautiful location, the reason for their being there temporarily forgotten. 'I've not been here before.'

'And it's nice and quiet,' Cassandra added. 'We won't be disturbed.'

Laura stared at the woman open-mouthed. 'You want to tie me up here?'

'Certainly. It's *much* more fun outside.'

'I...'

'Trust me, my dear; you'll love it.'

'But... but what if someone comes along?' Laura said, with little conviction.

The woman laughed quietly. 'It's unlikely. But if someone did, doesn't that idea turn you on even more?'

Laura opened her mouth to refute such a suggestion, and then paused. She really didn't fancy the idea... did she? Despite everything about the whole confusing episode unravelling around her, she had to admit that the prospect did secretly thrill her. Although she found it hard to acknowledge, the thought of being discovered in such illicit circumstances did actually excite her intensely. 'But nobody will come, will they?' was all she could say, her treacherous voice betraying a note of hope in the question.

Cassandra just smiled. 'Take your dress off, Laura,' she said.

Laura hesitated for a moment. What on earth was she doing in such a secluded place with such a strange, domineering woman? It didn't make any sense. She should walk away from Cassandra and go back to the house forthwith - shouldn't she?

But what then? What would she do? She had been craving some kind of excitement for ages and, standing in the peaceful secret clearing with Cassandra holding that cord, she felt more excited than she could remember ever feeling in her life.

Slowly, almost as though in a dream, her trembling fingers went to the buttons of her dress and she began to undo them, one by one. She kept her eyes lowered, unable to meet those of the housekeeper, aware of the slight smile that played about the woman's lips as she watched. She wondered briefly why Cassandra was going to such lengths; could it really be a purely altruistic act, or did she have some kind of ulterior motive? But all Laura knew at that moment was that the woman, and the books she'd read over the past few weeks, had kindled an awakening of her desires such as she had never dreamt possible.

She reached the last button and allowed the dress to slip from her and drop to the grass. Beneath it she wore a white bra and matching panties, and she looked questioningly at Cassandra, hoping she wouldn't have to go any further.

The woman surveyed Laura's lithe form with obvious approval, and then nodded. 'Very nice,' she said. 'Just slip the bra straps off your shoulders.'

Laura obeyed, relieved that she wasn't being asked to go any further.

'Now, put your hands behind you.'

'You'll stop if I ask you to, won't you?' she asked again, trying to reassure herself.

'I might,' the woman said; a different response from her previous one to the same question. 'But I won't harm you. You understand the difference, don't you?'

Laura nodded dumbly, although she was not sure of anything any more.

'Then put your hands behind your back.'

A slight hesitation and another anxious glance about, and then the beautiful girl obeyed, crossing her wrists just above her bottom. Cassandra touched her shoulders and turned her around, and then Laura inhaled sharply as she felt the cord bite into her flesh. 'Ow!' she complained.

'We must tie you tightly,' Cassandra replied calmly. 'Or it won't seem real.' She wrapped the cord twice around Laura's wrists and tied it tight, the last jerk making Laura's breasts quiver and inducing another uncertain protestation.

Once the wrists were secure Cassandra began binding the elbows, pulling them together, causing Laura's breasts to thrust forward even more than their normal youthful firmness permitted. Laura remembered how the tribesmen had done the same to the girl in one of the books, and how vulnerable her breasts

23

had been to the men's groping hands. The thought sent a sudden shiver of arousal coursing through her body - a shiver that was not missed by the hawk-eyed woman behind her.

'Turn around, Laura,' she ordered, when happy with her handiwork.

Laura obeyed, her cheeks glowing as she faced the housekeeper. She had never felt so vulnerable, standing as she was in the open air wearing only the skimpiest of underwear, her arms completely immobilised, totally at the mercy of the woman.

Cassandra reached into the bag again and pulled out a leather collar. It was studded, and there was a chain hanging from it. 'Hold up your head.'

Laura hesitated for a second, unsettled by the hardening tone of the woman, and then did as she was told, sensing it would be unwise to back out now. The woman fastened the collar about her throat, tightening it to a snug fit, then took the chain and tugged, watching with satisfaction as Laura staggered a little.

'Good,' she said, then casually reached out and ran a cold hand over her captive's breasts, her fingers tracing the edges of the bra and pressing into the soft creamy swellings above it.

'You're almost helpless now, little one,' she murmured, her eyes glued to the lovely flesh beneath her hand. 'Just how I want you.'

'W-what happens now?' Laura asked uneasily.

'Whatever I want,' came the reply. 'And first of all I want to see these delicious breasts of yours again.'

'But, what if someone comes along?' Laura protested, instinctively trying to back away from her tormentor. 'They'd see me without my bra on.'

Cassandra chuckled. 'I think we're a little beyond worrying about that, don't you?' she scoffed, easily holding Laura with the chain as though patiently dealing with a troublesome pet. Then with her usual ease of movement she reached behind Laura and unclipped her bra, savouring her squeal of dismay as the delicate garment dropped away, revealing the soft yet firm swelling of her breasts.

Laura closed her eyes and cringed, for she just new her traitorous nipples had hardened and now stood like small berries, as if in anticipation of the caresses that must follow.

'Mmm, you do have gorgeous breasts, little one,' murmured the housekeeper as she began to stroke them again. This time there was nothing Laura could do to stop her cold caresses. All she could do was stand there, her cheeks glowing as the woman indulged herself.

'You see how much more pleasurable it is when you're helpless?' she whispered. 'Just enjoy, my little one.'

Laura could not deny what the woman said was true. The discomfort and her helplessness caused by the bondage was having a quite inexplicable effect upon her and, as Cassandra continued to possess her breasts, she began to experience the same breathless arousal she had felt during their previous encounter. But then she only pretended to be tied. This was something very

24

different.

Cassandra lifted her hand to Laura's cheek, smoothing back her hair and gazing into her eyes. 'This is making you wet, isn't it?' she said.

Laura said nothing, but she knew her expression was telling the woman all she needed to know.

'Let's see how wet, shall we?'

'Please, no...' Again Laura's innocence and modesty made her want to resist, though she knew now that Cassandra would have her way. She wondered what was happening to her. What would her friends say and think, seeing her like this? And more to the point, what would her guardian say and think? But then, she had entered into the situation voluntarily and, despite her feeble protests, knew she wanted to be completely naked. Already in her mind she was the young woman in the African story, her clothes torn from her, forced to submit to the carnal desires of the savages who were her captors.

'Please...' she cried lamely as the woman eased her thumbs into the elastic of her panties, and then her knees almost buckled as the thumbs moved down and her panties whispered against her skin until they became a tiny white puddle around her feet.

Laura glanced down, her emotions in turmoil, her face red with shame, her body alive with excitement. Why was it that she found such treatment so arousing? Would any of her friends react in the same way? Would they be so shockingly turned on?

'Lean back against the tree and spread your legs, little slave girl,' Cassandra ordered, invading Laura's tormented thoughts with the complete assurance of one who knows she is in total command.

Without realising it Laura had been inched slowly backwards, and rough bark was now digging into her naked flesh. She looked into Cassandra's eyes, and then spread her legs, feeling a trickle of moisture escape from her vagina onto the pale smoothness of her thighs.

'You really are wet, aren't you, slave?' muttered Cassandra. 'Let me feel.'

'Yes... mistress,' Laura muttered instinctively. The form of address came out unbidden, yet sounded so right to her. She was the helpless slave, and Cassandra was her mistress, with complete control over her. A fresh shudder of arousal shook her as she contemplated this, and she felt the lips of her sex pulse with excitement.

Laura moaned softly, pressing her hips to the exploring hand, suddenly feeling an orgasm rise inside her as Cassandra moved her fingers slowly back and forth. The woman frigged her expertly, pressing her fingers deep into the heat of her sex, her thumb toying with the inflamed bud of her clitoris. Laura had forgotten all her inhibitions, her back pressed against the unyielding trunk of the tree and her pubis angled forward, her legs bent slightly as she abandoned herself to her desires. She was close to orgasm, and all she desired was that wondrous release.

But it was not to be that simple. The artful fingers withdrew, bringing a moan of disappointment from the aroused girl, who stared with wide pleading eyes at the woman. 'Mistress?' she whispered.

Cassandra held of her chin between thumb and finger, pulling her face to hers. 'You're really turned on, aren't you, my little slut?' she purred.

'Y-yes, mistress,' she gasped honestly.

'Good, because it's time to give you to a man, and to let you feel a real cock inside you.'

Chapter 6

Laura shook her head, convinced that she hadn't heard the woman properly. 'I... what did you say?' she asked.

'I said, it's about time you felt a real cock inside you,' the woman repeated sternly.

'But, I don't understand,' Laura objected feebly, her emotions still seething with unquenched desire.

'It's simple enough,' the woman said plainly. 'I'm going to have you fucked.'

Laura could not believe what she was hearing. 'But, my guardian is your boss,' she blurted without confidence, her head spinning from the shocking turn the encounter was taking. 'He'd be furious and sack you. You wouldn't dare do such a thing.'

'Oh, but you are so naïve,' Cassandra sighed with amusement, 'and so wrong. That's why I've arranged something a little different.'

Laura stared at her. 'What do you mean?' she gasped.

'Oh, don't worry, he's a personable looking chap,' Cassandra said airily, as though discussing nothing more than arrangements for a casual blind date. 'And he doesn't know who you are any more than you know who he is. It'll just be a fuck, with no complications.'

Laura shook her head and laughed, her eyes never leaving the woman standing before her. 'You... you can't be serious.'

'But of course I'm serious. I promised you I'd make things exciting for you, didn't I? Well, this is the next step. He's waiting at a quiet spot in the wood. Come on, I'll take you to him.'

'No, this has gone far enough,' Laura insisted, trying to resist the pull on the chain. 'Untie me and give me back my clothes, or I'll scream.'

'Scream all you want,' Cassandra mocked dismissively. 'I'll disappear into the trees like a shadow, and even if someone hears you, what are you going to tell them? That you undressed and tied yourself up accidentally? I really don't think so, do you?'

Laura glanced at her discarded but undamaged dress and underwear, then down at her nakedness. The damn woman was right; there was absolutely no way she could ever convince any possible saviour that she had been cajoled into such a predicament against her will, particularly if found totally on her own.

But she couldn't possibly go along with what Cassandra was suggesting. To submit her virginity to a stranger was unthinkable, but tied and unprotected as she was, it was outrageous.

Cassandra, though, was clearly not to be diverted from her plan. Heedless of Laura's protestations, she pulled the chain and began dragging her deeper into the wood. Laura tried to resist, but the collar bit into her neck and, with her arms immobilised, she had no choice but to stagger along behind, her breasts quivering with every uncertain step.

As they wound deeper into the trees Laura could not prevent her mind straying to the story of the helpless girl, captive and naked, being dragged through the forest by the rabble of natives, at their mercy, and a cold chill ran down her spine. But even as the girl's plight filled her mind, Laura felt a knot of delicious anticipation deep in her tummy.

The bondage and enforced nudity had already aroused her, and Cassandra's wily fingers almost delivered a glorious orgasm. Now, suddenly, the prospect of surrendering to a man was a very real one, and as she contemplated that fact she found her trepidations gradually giving way to a sense of breathless excitement. In her wildest flights of imagination she had never dreamed that one day her own plight would be so similar to that of the book's heroine. It was as if her deepest fantasy was coming true and, despite her chagrin, she struggled to deny her longing for it.

Eventually Cassandra stopped and turned to face her lovely plaything. 'He's just a little further ahead,' she said, and Laura felt a near overwhelming desire to turn and run. 'Now, you will not let me down. You will obey me fully. Understand?'

'But... but who is he?' Laura couldn't help but ask.

'That doesn't matter,' came the blunt reply. 'He doesn't know your name, and he doesn't know mine.'

'But, you're really expecting me to... to do it with a complete stranger?'

'That's what makes it all the more exciting.'

Laura lowered her eyes, unable to deny the accuracy of the woman's words. 'You won't leave me alone, will you?' she asked meekly.

Cassandra smiled. It was the smile of one who knew she had won, and Laura hung her head as she realised that she had signalled her acquiescence.

'Don't worry,' Cassandra said gently. 'I wouldn't miss this for anything. Now remember, there is no need for you to speak. All you have to do is obey.'

Laura nodded, accepting the inevitable.

'Good girl.' She tugged the lead once more, and Laura stumbled after her. There was a bend in the track ahead and as they turned it she saw the man, and her heart jumped into her mouth.

He was leaning against a tree, smoking a cigarette. Her mind was in such a spin she struggled to take it all in. He was a nothing to look at; someone eminently forgettable. His hair was mousy and not very neat, despite the warmth of the day he wore a coat that looked as though it needed a visit to the dry-cleaner, and faded jeans and a plain white shirt.

As the two approached he looked up, and his eyes widened as he devoured Laura's naked beauty. She felt the colour rise to her cheeks as his eyes crawled from her face to her breasts, then down to the dark nest between her thighs. Instinctively she tried to draw back, but Cassandra was having none of it, dragging her forward until she was standing in front of the stranger.

His expression gave way to a crooked grin as he surveyed the sexy girl in front of him. 'Hell, you weren't kidding,' he grunted to Cassandra, the cigarette wedged between his lips. 'She's fucking gorgeous.'

'I told you so.' Cassandra looked pleased with herself.

Laura listened in silence to the brief exchange, almost as if she wasn't there, or they were discussing some inanimate object rather than a person. Somehow though, if she was to get through the ordeal, she preferred it to remain that way. After all, how could she converse normally whilst naked with her hands pinned behind her and a collar about her throat? Better to be passive and to do as she was told.

Once again a tremor of arousal ran through her as these thoughts filled her mind. It seemed that obedience and passivity were what she was born for, and to be given naked and bound to a stranger in order to surrender her virginity was the right thing for the likes of her. To him she was merely an object, presented for his pleasure, just like the poor girls in the books.

'Open your legs,' ordered Cassandra, the sound of her voice bringing Laura back to the present. She looked at the housekeeper, then at the leering man, and a spasm of pure lust shook her. Somehow she wanted to part her legs, to flaunt her most private place to him. Lowering her eyes she placed her feet apart, only too aware of the moisture glistening on her dark nest.

The man studied her for a while longer, then stretched out a hand, palm up, and closed it over her sex. Laura moaned softly, her wantonness taking over as she pressed against the cupped palm. She knew how warm and wet she must feel, and then gasped as a finger penetrated her.

'She's hot as hell,' he murmured uncouthly, appreciatively. 'Look at her writhe about on my hand.'

Laura bit her lip, trying hard to keep her hips still as his coarse fingers slid in and out of her sex. She was barely in control now, her body totally alive with excitement as her fantasies unfolded in front of the housekeeper who had instigated them. She was the girl in the jungle, at the mercy of the lustful tribesmen. Or Belita, the girl held captive by the forest-dwellers. And as the man crudely fingered her wetness she began to recognise the true extent of the latent masochism that was simmering ever nearer to the surface.

'Does she suck?' he asked Cassandra, and once again Laura was struck by their complete disregard of her. Cassandra was in control, and Laura was no more than a passive slave; denied opinion, denied choice, denied the normal concessions to modesty any woman should expect.

Cassandra nodded. 'She will.'

'Then tell her to get on with it,' the man snapped gruffly.

'You heard him,' she said to Laura. 'Get on your knees.'

Laura was accustomed to Cassandra's authority, and again she obeyed, sinking to her knees, inhaling sharply as his fingers slipped from her vagina. Then she watched with a strange sense of detachment as the man undid the button on his jeans and slid down the zip.

Despite her naivety and lack of experience, she knew what was expected of her. Once again it was the books that had prepared her - instructed her - and she watched without a word of protest as the man rummaged inside his underwear and pulled out a semi-erect cock.

It was the first she had ever seen in the flesh, and it reminded her of some thick, pale sausage. He took it crudely in his fist and waved it in front of her emotionless face.

'Go on then,' he grunted, addressing her for the first time, 'open your mouth and suck, just like the lady said you would,' and he pressed the foreskin-covered glans against her lips a few times, demanding entry.

Laura knew the gruff stranger was not going to be denied, so taking a deep breath, she closed her eyes and opened her mouth, and the rigid flesh immediately stretched her lips wider and pressed inside. She hadn't known what to expect but she sucked tentatively, hoping it was the right thing to do. The demanding flesh felt strange as it pressed in, then withdrew until only the globular helmet was lodged between her lips. The man breathed heavily and shuddered a little, for a moment she marvelled at the effect she was having on him, and then the engorged column filled her mouth again until she thought she'd choke.

'Hell, she's not bad,' he said to the watching housekeeper. 'That's nice... very nice.'

His cock was fully erect now, filling her mouth, her lips stretched about its girth as she sucked with increasing endeavour. The feel and taste of it was extraordinary, sparking emotions in the innocent virgin that she had never imagined possible.

Totally carried away by the moment Laura worked harder, gliding her head back and forth, her hair and breasts swaying enticingly with her movements. She glanced up through lowered lashes, watching the intense expression on his face as he thrust his hips, his heavy balls rhythmically nudging her chin.

Then suddenly he swore and pulled back, his glistening erection disengaging from her mouth and bobbing in front of her wet lips. 'Hell, I'm almost there already,' he cursed. 'Get on your back before it's too late.'

As if in a dream, without question, Laura sank down into the soft, fragrant vegetation. At that moment she wanted to lose her virginity more than anything else, and she hurried to obey; a gesture of total surrender. He paused for a moment, staring down at her naked beauty, her breasts thrust upward by her trapped arms, and her sex glistening with moisture between her submissively parted thighs. Then he lowered himself to kneel between those toned limbs.

Laura closed her eyes as he took his cock in his fist, placed his other hand flat beside her flushed face to support his weight, and bent over her. She waited, wanting to feel that erect penis inside her; wanting to lose her virginity, no matter the circumstances, and when she felt it trying to gain entry she raised her bottom, willing him to penetrate her.

Laura gasped loudly as he stretched her. She wasn't afraid of pain; after all, despite her virginity she had accommodated that monstrous dildo, so she knew she could accept him.

He pushed harder and a cry escaped her lips as she felt him impale her with one smooth lunge of his hips. He grinned down triumphantly at her, his panted breath wafting over her face, his cock so deep their pubic hair entwined. He mauled her breasts, squeezing roughly, and sniggered when she winced as he pinched her tender nipples, enjoying her discomfort. Then he began to move, thrusting hard, arrogantly possessing her.

Laura was being fucked.

The ground was uncomfortable and her arms were stiff and numb beneath her, yet she didn't care; there was nothing but sensual delight for the submissive girl as the uncaring stranger took her virginity.

His thrusts became more erratic and less controlled, pounding her buttocks down on the ground, and she knew he was nearing his peak from the strained expression on his face, the bulging veins at his throat and temples, and the way his muscles trembled. She too was close to climaxing, but she lay inert beneath the panting, heaving onslaught, watching him through misty, fascinated eyes.

He came with a grunt, a dribble of saliva seeping from the corner of his slack lips, and for the first time in her life Laura felt a man's sperm pumping deep into her vagina. He erupted again, and again, and then she was coming too, whimpering into his shoulder as she was overwhelmed by pulse after pulse of pure, undiluted pleasure.

Some minutes later Laura opened her eyes. The man was gone, and the canopy of trees swayed and whispered overhead. Cassandra was standing over her, smiling down, the lead in her hand.

'Come on, little slave,' she said. 'Time to go home.'

Chapter 7

For the next few weeks the housekeeper left Laura alone, something for which she was profoundly grateful. Even the books ceased to appear, and she returned to the diet of classical literature to which, up until then, she had been accustomed. Superficially then, life reverted to normal at the house, with Laura returning to her routine of walks in the garden and afternoons spent sitting beneath a tree or, when it rained, in the drawing room, her face buried in a book.

Beneath the surface, though, things were far from normal for her. Her thoughts were dominated by memories of what had happened that afternoon in the woods, and how she had abandoned herself to pleasure, sacrificing modesty and dignity to satisfy the carnal pleasures the housekeeper had awakened inside her.

Still she could scarcely credit the way she had behaved, could barely believe it had happened. But it had, and she had been a willing, eager participant. The orgasm she experienced was real enough, and eclipsed anything she had experienced before. In fact, she had lain awake at night since the incident, reliving it in her mind, feeling once again the extraordinary excitement it had engendered. She caressed herself, teasing her breasts and her clitoris as the image of the man's cock filled her thoughts. Yet she had never since come close to the exquisite pleasures of that encounter.

Laura actually found herself seeking out the housekeeper during those long tranquil days. Although she feared the woman's power over her, she had awoken desires that Laura could never dream existed, and Laura felt inexorably drawn to her. But Cassandra proved elusive, and the only times that Laura had encountered her had been when her guardian and his wife or one of the other servants had been present. Even then she attempted to catch the housekeeper's eye, to communicate with her in some way, but without success. On the few occasions when their eyes did meet, she was able to read nothing in the woman's face.

Then one morning nearly three weeks after the encounter in the woods, Laura returned to her room after breakfast to find a new book lying on her pillow. At first she simply stared at it, almost unwilling to pick it up for fear of the effect it might have on her. But the more she hesitated the more she knew she needed to open it, so she snatched it up and headed for the garden.

She found a spot concealed from the house by a small copse. It was a favourite place of hers when she wanted some privacy. There was a bench set beside a hedge that always caught the sunshine in the mornings, and she settled upon it and opened the book.

It followed a familiar theme amongst Sir John's private collection; a beautiful girl kidnapped and forced to submit to the villains' whims. But this one was slightly different; this was more concerned with punishment. Page after page described how the wretched captive was stripped naked and whipped, how clamps were placed on her nipples and clitoris with weights attached, and how canes were used on her buttocks, breasts and belly, laying stinging stripes across her vulnerable flesh.

There were illustrations, too; pictures of the beautiful young woman tied in a number of breathtaking positions, and Laura was particularly struck by one of her hanging by her wrists, her legs tied wide apart while two men took it in turns to lash her naked buttocks.

Once again Laura was at a loss to understand her reaction to the book. The idea of physical punishment as an aphrodisiac was not one that had ever entered her mind, yet the accounts of the young woman submitting to the cruelty of her masters was having quite an unaccountable affect upon her.

She continued to turn the pages, staring at the pictures in awe. There was one of the girl stretched on a rack while a naked man fucked her. On the next page she was bent over a hurdle while a man laid about her with a cane, the stripes across her bare bottom lovingly picked out by the artist. It was all completely alien to Laura, yet extremely erotic, and she felt the familiar wetness seeping into her panties as she became more and more absorbed in the book.

'I thought that might fascinate you.'

Once again the housekeeper had caught Laura unawares, and she jumped at the sound of the enigmatic voice so close by. She looked up, squinting and trying to shade her eyes from the crisp morning sunlight, the housekeeper a slim black silhouette against the azure sky. 'What do you want?' she asked, already feeling a knot of anticipation in her stomach.

'I was looking for you,' the black figure said, nothing apparently moving. 'After all, you've been trying to seek me out for the last couple of weeks.'

'No I haven't,' Laura denied indignantly.

The silhouette chuckled lightly. 'Oh, but I think you have.'

'You must have imagined it,' Laura insisted defensively. 'Why would I want to see you, after what you've done to me?'

'Because you miss the books... and because you miss me and what I've awoken in you.'

'I - I don't know what you're talking about,' Laura snorted, unconvincingly.

The silhouette moved effortlessly and Cassandra sat next to Laura on the bench. 'All right, have it your own way,' she conceded pleasantly; the first time Laura could remember winning against her. 'How are you enjoying that one?'

'I, um, was just leafing through it,' Laura bumbled.

'Just leafing through it?' she laughed. 'You were totally absorbed in it, so much so that you haven't any idea how long I was standing there, have you?'

'I was distracted, that's all. And you always creep around; it's not surprising I didn't hear you.'

'And are you enjoying it?' the woman asked, ignoring the minor insult.

'It's all right, I suppose.'

'Which bits do you like the most? The whippings? The canings?'

'I... I don't know. I'm not sure I like any of it,' Laura said petulantly.

Cassandra smiled patiently. 'But you just said you do like it.'

'Cassandra,' Laura said, looking the woman in the eyes for the first time, 'what are you trying to do to me?'

'I just want to waken you up to yourself,' she said. 'Don't you want that?'

'I don't know. The other week, that was a terrible thing to do to me.'

'A terrible thing?' Amusement danced in Cassandra's eyes. 'But you loved it... all of it. And don't tell me anything different.'

Laura's cheeks reddened. 'You didn't give me much choice. I never would have agreed to go with you if I'd known that man was going to be there.'

'Which is precisely why I didn't tell you. As it was you responded beautifully, exactly as I knew you would.'

'I couldn't help it.' Her expression saddened. 'Cassandra, do you think there's something wrong with me?'

Cassandra put her cool hand on Laura's knee and laughed again. 'Of course there isn't. You're just learning about yourself, that's all. That's why I left that book in your room.'

Laura gazed down at the illustration on her lap. 'But nobody gets turned on by this sort of thing, surely?' she said.

Cassandra smiled inscrutably, but said nothing, leaving the girl to work it out for herself.

Laura shook her head. 'No,' she said. 'I couldn't accept anything like that.'

'So the pictures aren't turning you on?

'No.'

'Are you sure? You looked totally engrossed while I watched you.'

'I, um, was just amazed that such things might go on.'

'And not excited by the idea?'

'No. I mean, well, why should I be?'

'You tell me...' Cassandra spoke quietly, almost hypnotically, and her fingers inched, barely noticed, up Laura's smooth thigh, slipping beneath the hem of her cotton summer dress. 'Don't you think the idea of a cane biting into sweet bare flesh is erotic?'

'It, um, it can't be, can it?' Laura was getting increasing flustered, finding it difficult to concentrate as those cool fingers crept higher; crept higher without seeking permission.

'Just imagine it,' Cassandra went on quietly. 'Your wrists and ankles tied with cord, or silk, or leather. Your naked body suspended and helpless, your arms and legs stretched out and unable to move. Can you imagine it, dear Laura?'

The girl said nothing, but Cassandra watched with satisfaction as her eyes closed, and her breasts rose within the crisp cotton dress as she breathed deeply. She inched her fingers still higher, the tendons in the smooth thigh beneath them relaxed a little, and she savoured the girl's sweet exclamation as their manicured tips lightly brushed her panties. 'You're wet, Laura,' she whispered. 'The book turned you on, didn't it?'

'I... I suppose it did,' Laura admitted dreamily. The sensation of the fingers touching between her legs was beginning to drive all other thoughts from her mind as the passion inside her began to increase once more. What was it about the woman, she wondered, that brought out this side of her?

'Just imagine that's you, Laura,' the woman went on. 'Just imagine it's your pretty backside the men are thrashing. Think of that cane biting into your virgin flesh.' As she spoke her fingers were rubbing up and down the soft damp front of Cassandra's panties, pressing the delicate material against the sensitive lips of her sex and caressing over her love bud.

'Do you want to try it, Laura? the woman whispered. 'Do you want to be tied and caned?'

'I... I don't know.' Laura's hips were writhing slightly now, and the outline of her nipples pressed through the cotton dress, inviting the embrace of Cassandra's lips.

'We can do it, Laura,' the woman persisted. 'We can do it tonight.'

Laura was hearing the words but finding it increasingly difficult to concentrate on their portent. 'What... what do you mean?' she mumbled.

'I mean, we can do it. I know a place, and I have what we need.'

Laura inhaled sharply as the fingers moved expertly, her breasts swelling beautifully as her lungs filled with fresh morning air. 'You really want to do it to me?'

'Oh yes,' Cassandra purred, leaning closer and brushing her lips lightly over a little pulse in the delicious girl's throat. 'And you want me to.'

'Would... would there be anyone else there?' the entranced girl asked.

'There could be, dear Laura. Would you like that?'

'I don't know... who would it be?'

'A stranger. Like last time. Someone who you don't know, and who doesn't know you.'

'And I'd be caned?'

'Just like in the book.'

Laura opened her eyes and looked mistily at the woman, her mind in a complete spin. 'I'm not sure,' she whispered.

Chapter 8

The teeming rain lashed against the windscreen, the wipers, sweeping rhythmically back and forth, barely able to cope. The car's headlights picked out huge puddles of standing water, and great waves rolled to the sides as the wheels ploughed through them.

Laura gazed out into the evening light, wondering at the quantities of rain that were streaming down. The storm had been quite unexpected. One minute the evening was still and sultry, and the next the clouds rumbled in and the skies opened. She flinched slightly as a flash of lightning suddenly illuminated the scene around them, quickly followed by a crack of thunder.

Cassandra glanced across at her from the driving seat. 'Not afraid of thunder and lightning, are you Laura?' she asked breezily.

Laura shook her head. 'No,' she said distractedly, fingering the book in her lap, her eyes fixed on the road ahead.

Once again she was at a loss to understand what it was she was doing. How had she been persuaded to take such a trip? She should be safely in her room, precisely where her guardian thought she was, having made her excuses after dinner and retired pleading a headache. There she had awaited Cassandra, resolving to cry off; after all, the whole thing made no sense at all. Why should she be humiliated again at the hands of the housekeeper?

But, when she heard the quiet knock at the door she opened it and followed the woman down to the garage without a word.

Now they were driving through the storm. Laura had no idea where they were, or where they were going.

The car slowed and turned left. The headlights picked out nothing but trees, the track between them very narrow. Cassandra drove on for a few hundred yards, then stopped and put on the handbrake.

'Is this it?' Laura asked uneasily.

'We're not far away,' the woman replied. 'Now, we must take a few precautions. Turn away and put your hands behind you.'

From the tone of the woman's voice Laura knew she had to obey, and as she gazed at the rivulets streaming down the side window there was a click and something cold closed about her wrists. She tugged gently at the cuffs, but they held her arms securely.

'Good,' said Cassandra. 'Now hold your head still,' and Laura almost panicked as a black leather hood was tugged down over her eyes until it fitted closely over the bridge of her nose and across her cheeks. Then Cassandra tightened a strap at the back of Laura's head. 'Can you see anything?' she asked.

Laura shook her head and whispered, 'No.'

'No what?' came the terse prompt.

'Oh, um... no mistress.' Laura knew she had slipped into the submissive attitude Cassandra demanded. It was as if the bondage had once more changed her persona to that of a slave. Even now the sensation of the cold irons about her wrists and the loss of vision were sending little shivers of excitement through her. She was wearing a short halter-top without a bra, and she could feel her sensitive nipples pressing against the thin material as her excitement made them harden.

Cassandra put the car into gear and they moved off again, and a powerful sense of helplessness engulfed Laura. But it was not an unpleasant sensation; in fact, surrendering to Cassandra's will only served to increase her arousal as she tried to imagine where she was being taken.

They drove on in silence. The heavy pitter-patter on the roof and the rhythm of the wipers stopped and Laura knew it was no longer raining. Then at last the car turned sharply, and the crunch of gravel beneath the tyres told Laura they were in a private driveway.

Then Cassandra cut the engine. 'Stay there until you're called,' she ordered.

Laura sat alone in the car, her heart thumping, new doubts assaulting her. Where was she? Who else was there? Why had she been blindfolded? And why had Cassandra left her alone? She pulled at the cuffs, but they held her wrists with easy contempt. There was nothing she could do but sit and wait.

Long minutes passed, then she heard crisp footsteps on the gravel. They paused by the door, and then it opened.

'Listen Cassandra,' she blurted, 'I'm not too sure about...'

'Quiet!'

Laura squealed with shock and froze. It wasn't Cassandra; it was a man, and the aggressive manner warned her that no disobedience would be tolerated.

'Get out of the car.'

Laura hesitated for a moment. Then she swung a tentative foot out and climbed awkwardly from the vehicle.

'Stand still, legs apart.'

For a second Laura's instinct was to defy the voice, but she was alone, lost, bound and blindfolded. Her only hope lay in obedience, so she shuffled her feet a little apart and stood, her head high, waiting to see what would happen.

'Strip her.'

'Yes sir,' someone responded, and Laura jumped, thinking the man alone. Then she felt something cold and sinister against her shoulder - a knife - and she recoiled in horror, protesting loudly, only to yelp in anguish as something bit viciously through her thin skirt and panties, stinging her buttocks intensely.

'Stand still, I said,' growled the man.

Laura wanted to protest again, but thought better of it. She had no choice but to obey, and perversely, even as the thought struck a new spasm of excitement coursed through her. There was something extraordinarily exciting about the blow on her bottom, and for the first time she began to appreciate the depths of her masochism.

She felt the menacing blade against her shoulder once more, but this time she did not flinch.

It cut through the straps of her top with two swift movements. Then it slipped under the material at her waist, Laura shuddered as the cold steel pressed against her midriff, and then with one easy upward slice it cut cleanly through the top, from waist to cleavage. Laura felt the useless garment fall from her, and her face reddened beneath the mask as she knew the men were staring at her bare breasts.

Moments later the knife dissected her skirt, so that it too fell in tatters to the wet ground, and when it turned its attention to her panties she wanted to protest but knew it was futile, so she kept quiet, holding her breath as the elastic melted before the blade.

Laura was naked, trembling slightly, although the night was warm despite the rain.

Hands touched her neck and she recognised the feel of a leather collar. The chain dropped between her breasts, the cold metal making her tremble as it brushed her belly. Then someone tugged it.

She staggered along behind the man, her ears telling her that the other one was following. She had worn elegant high-heeled shoes that she knew showed off the shape of her legs. Now though, she regretted the decision, not just because of the difficulty in walking across the uneven surface of the drive, but also because of the way they drew attention to her nudity, their elegance in contrast to her total lack of clothing.

'Steps,' said the man tersely. They were stone, and then as they entered a building she was walking on wooden floorboards, her footsteps echoing unnaturally loud as she followed her captor.

They walked down a long corridor, and Laura heard voices getting louder. It was the hubbub of a social gathering, a dinner or a cocktail party. Conversations punctuated by laughter.

The sounds got closer, yet still the men drew her on. Then they turned and she just knew she was amongst the throng. The voices died, and she knew they were looking at her. A knot tightened in her stomach, and yet there was something incredibly exciting about being an exhibit, unknown to the unseen people admiring her. She was a naked slave, chained and brought before her masters for their amusement, forced to stand still while they scrutinised her. It was quite simply the most humiliatingly erotic thing that had ever happened to her. Her cheeks were hot with embarrassment as the ordeal continued, yet deep inside her arousal was growing with every second.

At last there was a tug on the lead and she moved forward. The sound of her heels seemed louder than ever as she walked from the room, and then the hubbub resumed.

They reached a staircase, and Laura stepped gingerly down the narrow flight, presumably to a cellar or something, and she shivered as cool air cloaked her naked body.

A door was unlocked, the bolts creaking as they were shot back. There was another tug, she stepped forward onto uneven flagstones, halted while the door was locked again, and then she felt fingers at the back of her head.

They unbuckled the mask, pulled it off, and the light made her flinch. She blinked, trying to focus, then gazed around. She was indeed in a cellar, with grisly chains hanging from iron rings set in the stone walls. It was lit by a stark strip light that filled its centre with a cold, cheerless glare, but was unable to penetrate the baleful shadows on the fringes. There were a number of contraptions set about the floor, each with more chains, and against one wall was a rack of canes and whips, the sight of which sent an icy shiver down Lisa's spine.

She looked at the men. The one holding the lead was middle-aged, with dark hair greying at the temples. He had a craggy face with deep-set eyes. His companion was slightly younger with a shaven head, his beady eyes crawling over her nakedness.

The older of the two raised a hand and cupped her breast. She tried to shy away, but his companion grasped her shoulders, holding her steady while the first man mauled her.

'What a pretty little thing you are,' he murmured. 'I'm going to enjoy putting some stripes across that lovely arse of yours. You do know that's what you're here for, don't you?'

Laura's mouth was dry and she simply could not speak, but her anguish seemed to please the man. He smiled and spoke to his companion, his eyes never leaving hers. 'The frame, I think,' he said.

'Wh-where's Cassandra?' Laura managed to blurt. 'I-I thought she'd be here.'

The man chuckled dismissively, making her wince as he pinched her nipple. 'We'll not need her. Now don't speak out of turn, or it'll be the worse for you.'

Laura was in a blur of conflicting emotions as the bald man guided her to an upright wooden frame, made of stout oak beams with chains attached to each corner. Laura was made to stand in its centre while he undid her cuffs.

Her freedom was short-lived, for no sooner had he removed them he grabbed her right hand, pulled it up to the top corner of the frame and clamped a manacle about her wrist. He did the same with the other, leaving her with her arms stretched above her head. Next he pulled her ankles apart and clamped heavy shackles to them. These were attached to more chains, which they tightened, stretching her naked form into an X-shape.

Laura had never felt so vulnerable, and she watched the two men with apprehension as they eyed her. Not for the first time she wondered what she'd let herself in for. In her current situation she was totally unable to protect herself. The men could do what they wanted, and she was completely powerless to stop them.

And yet, despite her fear, another emotion was already becoming dominant. One that, until recent events, she would scarcely have believed possible. It was a sense of sexual arousal such as she had never before experienced. Ever since the cuffs and blindfold were deployed in the car, Laura had felt an intense excitement rising within her, and now her entire being was alive with anticipation.

The men turned away to a rack that was hung with canes of varying thicknesses. They selected a few, cutting them through the air, and Laura held her breath, unable to tear her eyes away. She thought of the effect they would have on her poor bottom, and her knees crumbled as the two onerous men prepared for her forthcoming punishment with elaborate deliberation.

Chapter 9

At last they were ready. They chose a vicious-looking cane, no thicker than her index finger. The older man flexed it as they approached her again, and Laura felt a cold sensation in her stomach as she watched it, eyes wide.

The man stretched out his arm and touched the implement against her flank. Laura flinched as the wood contacted her flesh, but she was unable to avoid it and the man ran the tip down the side of her body, tracing the curve of her breast, her waist, the swell of her hip, then sliding it over the strained tendons of her thigh.

'Right, sweet little slut,' he said quietly. 'Now we must explain the rules of our little game to you.'

'R-rules?' stammered Laura.

'That's right. We have to make it an enjoyable experience for everyone.'

'Everyone? I don't understand.'

'The little party you were introduced to upstairs,' the man explained calmly. 'They have very good reason for taking a personal interest in your punishment.'

Laura stared at him. Just what had Cassandra lured her into? She had agreed to the chastisement, certainly, but she hadn't imagined that it would be anything more than that. Now, though, it appeared that something more elaborate was planned for her.

'Let me explain,' he went on. 'It's all really quite simple. The guests upstairs are here not just to witness your punishment, but to take a hand in it.'

Laura was mortified. 'You mean, they're going to beat me?' she whimpered.

The man smiled and nodded. 'Now you're beginning to get the point.'

'All of them?'

He shook his head. 'This is no randomly selected group of people,' he said. 'There are precisely twenty men and twenty women. Even as we're speaking they are drawing lots. Each man will receive a number between one and twenty, as will each woman, and nobody discloses what number they've drawn at this stage.'

'But, what do the numbers mean?' Laura felt compelled to ask, even though she dreaded the answer.

'For the women they denote which stroke they will lay across that pretty behind of yours. Number one has the first blow, number two the second, and so on.'

'Twenty?' gasped Laura. 'I'll never take twenty. I couldn't.'

'And that's the beauty of it,' he went on with a smile. 'You see, the sight of your exquisite beauty will of course make all the men want to fuck you. However, as each blow is struck, the man with the corresponding number drops out.'

'S-so, each stroke I take means one less man?'

'That's right. However, we anticipate that you'll beg for mercy long before the twentieth stroke is laid across your bottom, and when that happens, whichever men are left will be allowed to fuck you.'

Laura's mouth dropped open as comprehension dawned. 'You mean...'

'Yes,' he smiled with satisfaction, 'if you're weak it could be quite a long night for you.'

She stared at him incredulously. 'But you can't,' she gasped. 'I mean, I just couldn't...'

'At this moment you don't have any choice,' he said. 'We make the rules, and you will abide by them.'

'But...'

'Now, it's important you know all the rules,' he went on, cutting her off. 'Once the punishment has begun, only by saying the words "I surrender" will you be able to stop it. Then the remaining men will redeem their prize.'

'I won't let them,' she said, her voice shaking.

'I'm afraid you'll have no choice,' he replied. 'That frame is an ingenious device. We can manipulate your body to make you available to them without even having to unshackle you.'

'You mean, they'll take me here, with everybody watching?' she wailed.

'Naturally. After all, the men who don't get to sample you directly will want some kind of consolation.'

Laura was flabbergasted. It was the most fiendish plan imaginable. Not only was she to be whipped but, should she prove unable to take the punishment, she was to submit to the humiliation of being publicly screwed. And there was nothing she could do to prevent it.

'Wait a minute,' she protested. 'Someone might recognise me, and I was promised anonymity.'

'Don't worry about that, my dear,' said her captor. 'We've thought of that. Nobody will recognise you.'

He nodded to his companion, who reached into a pocket and pulled out another black mask, but this one had eyeholes. He placed it over Laura's head and buckled it tight behind her head, then stepped back.

'There,' said the man in charge. 'Isn't that better? Just take a look.' As he spoke his assistant moved a full-length mirror out from the shadows, and positioned it so that Laura was afforded a perfect view of herself. The hapless girl was both shocked and excited by the sight she made, her lithe body stretched and open, her breasts jutting forward, the nipples standing proudly erect.

With the mirror in position a table was placed beside it. It was narrow, with two rows of holes at each end, and each hole was numbered from one to twenty. But Laura barely had time to consider their implication before the man in charge began to speak once more.

'So what do you think?' he asked. 'I just know they're really going to enjoy thrashing you, but the point is, how many strokes can you take?'

'Or,' put in the thuggish assistant, sniggering, 'how many cocks?'

Just then the cellar door creaked open and the guests filed in. Laura wanted the floor to open and swallow her up as she watched them. The women came first, their evening gowns a striking contrast to Laura's nudity, and their relaxed demeanour serving only to increase her tension as she considered the disgraceful sight she made.

They made their way to Laura's left, each clutching a small white ball, and Laura guessed that these were fiendish lottery balls that would govern the order in which they were to beat her.

Once the women were gathered the men shuffled in. They were quieter than their partners, each fixing his gaze on Laura's beauty, the tension between them obvious.

The heavy door closed with an eerie finality, and the man addressed them.

'Welcome ladies and gentlemen,' he began. 'As you can see, our lovely young guest has been prepared for the evening's entertainment. In keeping with the rules of this establishment, she is not a professional and is being paid nothing for her part in tonight's proceedings. I have explained our little game to her, and she understands fully. She also knows how to stop the game and the consequences for doing so.'

Laura simply did not know what to think. She was extremely anxious, but extremely turned on too. She was nothing more than a plaything to entertain the guests - and that reality alarmed and excited her with equal measure.

'As always, nobody has disclosed the number he or she has drawn to anyone else,' the man went on. 'This means we don't know which of our esteemed male guests,' he smiled politely at them, 'will drop out when each of our lovely female guests,' he smiled and bowed a fraction, 'lands a blow. So much more interesting that way, don't you think?'

There was a murmur of agreement.

'Now,' he went on, 'may I ask which lady has ball number one?'

A woman raised her hand and stepped forward, then placed the ball into the similarly numbered hole on the table beside the mirror, the number clear for all to see.

The woman then moved to where the helpless girl was tethered, eyeing her with an expression of amusement. She accepted the cane from the man and ran her fingers along its length, then took a couple of practice swings, the sound of the thin rod cutting through the air making the naked girl's stomach churn with dread and anticipation.

The room fell completely silent, the main man nodded, and the woman drew back her arm.

Swish! Whack!

The cane descended with terrible force onto the bare flesh of Laura's unprotected bottom. For a second she was numb, then the pain bit, inducing a muffled yelp as the stripe laid by the cane darkened to a deep red colour.

Laura clenched her teeth, trying to blot the pain from her mind as the woman handed the cane back. A man detached himself from the group on Laura's right and placed his ball into the corresponding hole on his side of the table, before moving to the fringes with the woman who had struck her. It was outrageous; they were playing a form of bingo for her!

But she barely had time to dwell on this before a second woman detached herself from the group and placed her ball in its spot. Then she gripped the cane and drew back her arm.

Swish! Whack!

The second blow struck with even greater force than the first, striking her high on her nether cheeks, the end of the cane wrapping about her shapely hips and cutting into the softness of her flawless flesh. It was all Laura could do to suppress a scream as the dreadful agony of the stroke overwhelmed her, bringing tears to her eyes.

A second man, older than the first, placed his ball in its hole, and the pair joined the other two. Then a third woman gripped the cane in her fist, a grim look of intent etched on her face.

Time became a blur of pain to the hapless girl. Over and over the ritual was repeated, a woman placing her ball in position then taking up the cane. None showed the smallest inkling of mercy as they brought it down ruthlessly across Laura's stinging buttocks, before retiring with a male counterpart to the shadows.

After ten strokes there was a lull, and Laura was allowed to recover some composure. The panting girl was writhing feebly in her bonds, her body coated with a sheen of perspiration as she fought to deny the fiery discomfort in her haunches, but as she gazed through lowered lashes at her dishevelled reflection, a spasm of lust shook her bound frame.

She eyed the men who waited, and in particular their tented suit trousers. Clearly each of them craved her, and she knew she must summon all her resolve to deny them. But she wondered if she could stand another stroke of the cane, and when the next woman stepped forward she groaned with dismay.

Swish! *Whack*!

This time she screamed as the flexible cane swept into her throbbing backside with a pain like the stinging of a thousand wasps.

Swish! *Whack*!

She writhed, twisting and contorting, her breasts quivering as she tried in vain to avoid the brutal implement.

Swish! *Whack*!

Her pitiful protestations echoed about the cellar as the agony of the beating continued. She knew she could take little more, but the sight of seven men still waiting was incentive enough to hold out as yet another woman picked up the cane.

Swish! *Whack*!
Swish! *Whack*!
Swish! *Whack*!

The onslaught became too, too much, and Laura could take no more. '*Please*... I surrender!' she wailed.

The man in charge imperiously raised a hand and moved closer to the defeated girl. 'What did you say?' he asked.

'I... I surrender,' she repeated feebly, her voice a mere whisper as she hung slack in her bonds.

There was a murmur of excitement from those watching, but Laura didn't care. She simply let her body go limp, the manacles cutting into her wrists as they took the full weight. She looked through tear-blurred eyes at the four men still clutching their tokens, but couldn't discern their faces, which didn't seem to matter any more. At least the chastisement had stopped, and the thought of surrendering herself to them seemed trivial compared to the prospect of another blow of the cane.

To Laura's relief they didn't immediately carry out the next phase of her ordeal. Instead they all filed from the room, leaving her alone, slowly regaining some composure.

As she recovered her mind cleared too, and the full import of what was happening to her returned. Her torment was far from over, she knew. A punishment was one thing, but to be screwed by four strangers was quite another. And to perform in front of others was another still. When she blurted her surrender there was nothing but pain motivating her. Now though, given time to contemplate the import of her capitulation, she cursed her weakness. Surely she could have taken just four more strokes?

Yet the eroticism of her situation didn't escape her either. The exposure and humiliation of the chastisement had already heightened her state of arousal and, despite everything, she savoured the anticipation whilst contemplated what was to come next. She thought of the girl in the book she'd been reading only that morning, and of the cruelty of her captors. The idea had excited her then, was doing so tenfold now, and she wondered at the perversity of her desires.

By the time the people returned Laura had recovered well. She stood, her back straight, her head held high, her bare breasts jutting proudly, the nipples still erect. She watched as the guests gathered, and then the main man was beside her once more, clutching her chin between thumb and forefinger and pulling her head round to face him.

'Now then, my dear,' he said. 'The pain is over. Now comes the pleasure.'

'Must I do it with all these people watching?' she asked plaintively.

'Oh, absolutely,' he replied. 'That's all part of the fun for my guests. Besides, I know it will give you a thrill too.' With total confidence he lowered his hand and cupped her breast, and smiled at her obvious delight as he teased the stiff nipple. 'I've seldom seen a captive so responsive,' he remarked. 'I'm sure you'll enjoy this as much as we will.'

Meanwhile his thuggish companion positioned something in front of Laura. It was a low bar, like a stout hurdle level with her crotch, and he placed it so that the wooden bar pressed against her pubis. As he did so the man in charge withdrew two metal pins from the uprights on the frame and, to Laura's surprise, the whole upper half began to pivot forward on strong hinges, so that she moved with it until bent forward over the hurdle, her bottom raised, her hands stretched out in front of her. Despite her appalling predicament, the thought of her vulnerability made her breathless with exhilaration.

There was a slight commotion, and Laura strained to see the four men with the winning tokens had entered. Each was dressed in a white bathrobe, and they filed round to stand in front of their prize, their eyes fixed on her.

'Right, gentlemen,' said the main man. 'Here is your prize. You may use her as you wish.'

Barely had the words left his lips than the first of the men slipped under the top bar of the frame and straightened up in front of her. He was no picture; quite stout and losing his hair. He was hardly the type she would have chosen, but choice was a luxury she no longer enjoyed. When he slipped off the bathrobe, however, Laura's attention was diverted to the circumcised cock that hung from his groin. It dangled just in front of her face, and when he gripped her head and raised it she knew precisely what he wanted, so she opened her mouth and accepted his cock.

She sucked gently, and immediately it began to swell, stretching her lips wider apart and making her suddenly eager to feel it at full stiffness.

The man grunted and reached down for her breasts, crushing them and drawing small moans from her as she continued to suck him. He was soon fully erect, almost making her gag as he pressed to the back of her throat.

Then to her amazement he withdrew, slipped away, and was immediately replaced by a second man. He too dropped his robe, revealing a hairy chest and a long, semi-hard cock that he immediately fed into Laura's mouth, so that she was obliged to begin sucking once more.

Scarcely had she taken him between her lips, however, than she felt something smooth and slippery pressing against her wet sex. She was about to be fucked, and was suddenly transported by a flood of desire as he forced his stiff erection into her, until she winced at the sensation of his wiry pubic hairs brushing against the tender flesh of her freshly thrashed backside.

He began to fuck her with long easy strokes. Laura groaned around the flesh in her mouth as his belly slapped against the taut skin of her bottom, each slap making her squeeze her eyes shut. But the discomfort was rapidly being eclipsed by the pleasure as she revelled in the wonderful sensation of the stiff cock pumping in and out of her.

The harder he fucked, the more excited she became, and the more enthusiasm she showed as she sucked greedily at the cock in her mouth. Laura was being rocked back and forth, the frame creaking, her breasts swaying as she revelled in the sheer debauchery of what they were forcing her to do.

Then her attention was drawn back to the cock possessing her mouth, which suddenly jetted thick, creamy liquid into her throat. Instinctively she swallowed as he filled her mouth with his copious ejaculation, tasting male seed for the first time, feeling a little seep from the corners of her lips and down her chin.

He kept his cock buried in its warm moist sanctuary, and scarcely had she swallowed the last of his sperm when the cock rutting deep inside her cunt erupted too.

Then Laura was coming, her hips undulating in a lewd dance of lust as the sensation of his orgasm sent her over the top. Her face reddened in shame as she heard those watching comment on the violence of her orgasm, but she had lost all control, convulsing with undiluted delight as wave after wave of pleasure coursed through her.

The beating and the sheer strength of her orgasm had taken it out of her, and Laura slumped, all energy drained from her. She felt the men withdraw and closed her eyes, wanting only to sleep. But they hadn't finished with her, and she moaned wearily as another erection prodded against her sex lips and sank into her vagina, and a forth wormed persistently into her aching mouth.

The next few minutes were a blur. After frenzied rutting the men ejaculated and she responded with a shattering orgasm, though she had no idea from where she summoned the energy.

Then the basement was emptying, the onlookers' murmurs of approval fading up the cellar steps. Hands released the bonds and lowered her to the floor, and there Laura lay, tired and aching, scarcely knowing or caring what was going on.

And then she became aware of a stiletto shoe just in front of her face, and let her eyes travel up the slender leg and on to the cool eyes that stared down at her.

Cassandra smiled, a mocking smile.

'That was quite a performance, Laura,' she said. 'I can see you're a fast learner.'

Chapter 10

Once again Cassandra allowed Laura some time to recover after that night. Laura was grateful and spent the next two days in bed, for the sake of her guardian feigning a bad cold, while the housekeeper tended to her needs. Lying on her front, on her own, Laura found time to reflect on what she had done, and on what she was becoming, and the contemplation left her confused.

She could scarcely believe she had allowed it all to happen, and yet the memory, whilst bringing shame, also brought back the acute arousal she had secretly savoured during the ordeal.

During her short convalescence she scarcely spoke to Cassandra, watching the housekeeper going about her business. Twice a day, however, the woman would bring in a jar of ointment and Laura would lie on her stomach, her nightgown pulled up while the woman rubbed the cool unction into the tender flesh of her buttocks. As she caressed, the woman would trace the marks that still criss-crossed her bottom, remarking upon them.

'This one was made by Mrs M,' she would say. 'I could see she really enjoyed thrashing you. And here's the mark made by Mrs J. She never was much good at aiming, that's why it's across your back.'

On the third day Laura got out of bed, and though sitting down was still uncomfortable, she managed to hide her discomfort and returned to the garden as if nothing had happened.

She was dozing in the warm sun when the shadow of the housekeeper falling across her face woke her. She blinked up at the older woman.

'May I join you?' the housekeeper asked.

Laura eyed her warily. 'I suppose so,' she acquiesced.

Cassandra sat down. 'How are you feeling?'

'I'm okay. Still a bit sore.'

'I'm not surprised. That was quite a thrashing you took. Most people expected you to call a halt at a dozen at most.'

'And have eight men...?' Laura's voice tailed off as she found herself unable to speak the words.

'Have eight men fuck you?' Cassandra finished her sentence with confident ease. 'You seemed to be responding pretty well to the four who did.'

'I couldn't help it,' Laura mumbled shamefully.

Cassandra put a hand on her knee. 'No, you couldn't, could you? You're a sensual creature, Laura, and you mustn't fight the fact.'

Laura shivered slightly at the touch. She knew the conversation was leading to something, though she didn't know what. The thought that Cassandra had something new in store for her brought a slightly sick feeling to her stomach, yet already she could feel the excitement begin to rise as she pondered what her new mentor might have in mind. 'What do you want from me, Cassandra?' she asked.

'Want?' the woman mocked. 'Why should I want anything? I just dropped by for a chat.'

'Yes, and every time you do you make me do something outrageous,' Laura pointed out. 'Why should this time be any different?'

'Well, it is different. In fact, I was just going to ask if you'd like to play a little game with me.'

Laura eyed her suspiciously. 'What kind of game?'

The woman laughed and casually tossed her hair back in the sunshine. 'A card game, that's all,' she said, her gaze returning to hold Laura's, the humour disappearing from them.

'What card game?' Laura asked suspiciously.

'Poker. Well, strip poker, admittedly.'

Laura shook her head. 'I might have known. There's always something sexual with you.'

Cassandra squeezed her knee. 'And that's why you like me so,' she said, and then rose. 'I'll be in the garden shed,' she said. 'Meet me there in fifteen minutes.' Then, without waiting for an answer, she walked away, her hips swaying elegantly.

Laura watched her go. Already the sinking feeling in her stomach was increasing, though she couldn't quite understand why. There was something about Cassandra's attitude, her air of authority, which excited the youngster more than she cared to admit. It was clear that she expected Laura to play her game. There had been no attempt at persuasion, just a calm invitation. Laura wondered what she could be up to. A simple game of strip poker couldn't be all she had in mind. Perhaps she should simply not turn up. That would teach the arrogant woman a lesson, wouldn't it? Yet, as the minutes ticked by, she found herself glancing again and again at her watch and, ten minutes after the woman had left, she rose and made her way down towards the copse, behind which stood the large shed.

As she placed a slightly trembling hand on the shed doorknob she glanced around to make sure nobody was watching. Then she pushed the creaking door open and stepped inside. It was dingy and warm and stuffy, and smelt of creosote and oil, and amongst the tools and bags of compost and bulbs, was a small table behind which Cassandra sat, shuffling cards.

'Ah, there you are,' she said, glancing up. 'Take a seat... or should I say,' she added with a chuckle, 'take a pile of sacks?'

'I'm not sure about this,' said Laura, glancing about. 'What are you up to, Cassandra?'

'I'm not up to anything,' the woman said, and elaborate expression of mock hurt on her face. 'Just looking for a little harmless fun to pass the time, that's all.'

Laura looked around the shed uneasily. 'There's nobody else here, is there?'

'Nobody. Just us. Now sit down and we'll cut for dealer. You know how to play, don't you?'

Laura nodded. She had learnt the game at school. She hadn't been very good then, and she wasn't confident she'd be any good now.

At first the game seemed to be going Laura's way. Cassandra lost both her shoes in the first two hands, and when Laura laid down two pairs at the end of the third she was delighted to see the woman reach hesitantly for the buttons on her blouse, and watched with interest as the garment was peeled off. The woman's breasts were encased in a black bra that lifted them delightfully, enhancing her cleavage, and Laura blushed as she found herself taking an interest in the woman's body, her eyes being drawn constantly back to her very inviting breasts. There was something undeniably sexy about her, and Laura shifted uncomfortably on her sacks.

Then the game began to swing in Cassandra's direction. Laura quickly lost her shoes. Then she too was peeling off her top. In the next game she lost her skirt and felt very conspicuous indeed, sitting in her lacy white bra and panties, waiting for Cassandra to deal the cards.

She picked up her hand and examined it. Two tens, a three, a five and a queen. Keeping hold of the tens, she threw down the other three cards and waited while Cassandra dealt her replacements. When she picked them up her heart jumped. Two tens and a four. That meant she had four tens. She couldn't lose.

Keeping her face as straight as she was able she glanced at Cassandra, who was examining her own cards. She discarded two, replacing them from the pack. Then she looked at Laura.

'Well?' she prompted.

'I'll go two, I think.'

'Two?' the woman scoffed. 'That's your bra and knickers.'

'That's right,' Laura said confidently, her nose held defiantly high.

'Okay. Your two, and raise you two.'

Laura glared at her. 'All right, here are your shoes and blouse back.'

Cassandra cocked her head to one side. 'Oh no,' she said, wagging a finger at the girl, 'once we've lost our clothes we can't have them back.'

'I know, but I've got nothing else to bid with,' Laura protested.

Cassandra thought for a while. 'All right, just this once then,' she said. 'But that means I can bid with your clothes too. So I'll raise you two more.'

Laura cursed silently. It was her best hand yet and she badly wanted to win back her clothes, but she had nothing left to bid with. 'Could I get a credit?' she asked.

'What kind of a credit?'

Laura shrugged. 'I don't really know,' she admitted. 'Just some kind of a credit, that's all.'

'Well, okay,' Cassandra said, 'but if you lose you have to do a forfeit.'

'What do you mean?'

'I don't know, something exciting.'

Laura felt her stomach tighten; she saw a glint in Cassandra's eye that made her suddenly nervous, and she sensed she was being lured into some kind of a trap. 'I... I couldn't take another caning,' she said. 'I'm still too sore.'

'Oh, I think we can find something else for you to do,' replied Cassandra, and then she suddenly beamed. 'I've got it!' she declared with an enthusiasm that belied her usual austerity. 'If my hand beats yours you have to walk back to the house naked.'

'No,' Laura shook her head vigorously. 'No, I couldn't do that!'

'Why not? You've been naked in front of others before, like at the club the other night.'

'That was different,' Laura said indignantly. 'Nobody there knew me.'

'So it's okay to be seen naked by strangers, but not by people who know you?'

'It's different, and you know very well what I mean.'

'All right, you have to walk naked through an area where there'll be strangers,' Cassandra conceded.

Laura shook her head again. 'I couldn't. No, not naked.'

'Well, wearing just bra and knickers, then.'

Still Laura shook her head.

'Then you can't be confident that your hand's any good,' Cassandra pointed out smugly. 'And remember, if you don't respond to my bid you lose anyway.'

Laura looked down at her cards. The housekeeper was right. She stood to lose if she didn't bet the forfeit - and she had four tens! Surely she'd win, and have the pleasure of getting one over on the housekeeper. 'I'd definitely be allowed to wear my underwear?' she asked for confirmation.

'Definitely.'

Laura grit her teeth, and made her mind up. 'All right,' she said. 'I'll see you.'

Cassandra smiled slyly, and then lowered her hand to the rough table.

She was holding four jacks.

Chapter 11

Laura sat in the passenger seat of Cassandra's car. She could scarcely believe that, so soon after the incident at the club, she would once again be at the mercy of the housekeeper. She cursed her stupidity in believing that she could possibly manage to get one over the scheming woman.

She looked at the clock on the dashboard. Nine forty-five. At least it was beginning to get dark. And that was something she needed, considering the way she was dressed. She felt the blood rush to her cheeks as she thought about the sight she would make that evening.

Cassandra had come for her at nearly nine o'clock. Her guardian and his wife were at a function and would not return until late, making Laura feel even more vulnerable than usual. She had followed Cassandra down to her quarters, where the woman led her into her sitting room and closed the door. 'Are you ready for this, Laura?' she asked. 'You remember the agreement?'

Laura nodded.

'Excellent,' the woman said. She held out a hand, and what appeared to be a flimsy piece of red material.

'What's this?' asked Laura.

'It's what you're going to wear during your little stroll.'

'But I've already got my underwear on.'

'So take it off,' and before Laura could protest she found herself led into the bedroom and left alone, the door being closed behind her.

She sat on the bed and examined the red underwear. It was made of the sheerest see-through silk imaginable.

There was a knock at the door. 'Come on Laura, you ready yet?' Cassandra called, a hint of impatience in her tone.

'In a moment,' Laura called back, and with a pout of reluctance she rose to her feet and began unbuttoning her dress.

The headlights picked out a building, and the car slowed. It was a small country pub, and the sign outside proclaimed it as the *Red Dragon*.

'See this place?' said Cassandra. 'That's where I'll be waiting for you. The car will be in the car park with the door unlocked until eleven fifteen. If you're not with me by then I'll drive home without you. All right?'

'All right,' said Laura quietly.

The car began to pick up speed again, and Laura stared from the window with sinking spirits; she knew the next time she passed this way she would be alone and on foot. Worse still, she would be practically naked.

They drove on. For the most part the road was a quiet country lane but, about a mile from the pub they passed through a village, its main street illuminated by streetlights, and Laura felt even more unnerved as she realised she would have to find her way through without being seen.

Shortly afterwards the car began to slow, and Laura saw another pub ahead.

This time Cassandra turned into the car park and drew to a halt, extinguishing the headlights. She turned to Laura. 'This is it,' she said. 'Come on inside and I'll buy you a glass of Dutch courage.'

Laura climbed grudgingly from the car and followed the woman on legs that felt decidedly wobbly.

The pub was warm and busy. Cassandra made her way to the bar and, without asking Laura what she wanted, ordered two large malt whiskies. She then led Laura to a cosy table in the corner and handed one to her. 'Here, drink that,' she said. 'It'll calm the nerves, believe me.'

Laura sipped the drink. It was smooth and warmed her throat. She took another sip.

'Good, isn't it?' said Cassandra, and then placed her hand on top of Laura's. 'Feeling excited?'

'I...' Laura's voice trailed away. As usual Cassandra had read her like a book. During the journey in the car her main emotion had been fear. Now though, as she took another sip of her whisky, she realised for the first time that she was actually feeling excited... very excited. And the more she thought about what she was about to do, the greater was her excitement.

Cassandra smiled and gently, almost absent-mindedly, caressed the back of Laura's hand as it lay on the table. 'My goodness, you're an odd one,' she murmured. 'Now finish your drink and let's get started.

Laura avoided her eyes, swallowing down the last of the fluid, enjoying the warmth that permeated her body.

As she made her way out of the pub Laura was aware of the many pairs of hungry male eyes upon her shapely form. She knew the short dress hugged her curves, and that there was scarcely a man in the place who wouldn't want to get her out of it. She wondered what their reaction would be if they had any idea what she was about to do.

They stepped out into the deepening twilight. The air was warm, the sky glowing orange as the summer sun approached the horizon. She followed Cassandra towards the car, her steps becoming more and more hesitant as they drew close to it.

Then Cassandra turned to face her and held out a hand. 'The dress please,' she said severely, her tone once again forthright.

Laura looked around hesitantly. The car park was well lit, but there was nobody in sight. Tentatively she began undoing the buttons on the dress one by one. She reached the bottom button and stood, holding the garment together and glancing around once more. Then she pulled it back, let it slide down her arms, and handed it to Cassandra.

The housekeeper let her eyes travel down Laura's body, lingering on her breasts, which the girl knew were virtually naked within the wispy bra. Then she smiled.

'Well, I'll see you at the *Red Dragon*,' she said. 'And remember, eleven-fifteen, not a second later or you're on your own.'

As she spoke a car swung in off the road, its lights bright. Instinctively Laura ducked down beside Cassandra's car, but already the woman had climbed inside and was starting the engine. Moments later the vehicle was on the move, leaving Laura alone and exposed in the middle of the car park. She saw the people emerging from the newly arrived car, hesitated for no more than a second, and then she was running for the road.

Chapter 12

Laura's attempt to run in her heels was doomed to failure, and it seemed to take forever to find any form of cover. Only when she was a fair distance from the pub did she dare look back to see if she was being followed. When she did she gave a sigh of relief; clearly the occupants of the car had failed to spot her and, for the moment, she was relatively safe in the deserted road.

To her left was a hedge that ran along the edge of a field. It was tall and without breaks, and would offer her little chance of cover if she needed any in a hurry. On her right was a deep wide ditch, beyond which was a high fence, beyond which was a wood. That's where she wanted to be, but there was no sign of a gate or a breach in the barrier that separated her from it. With a sinking feeling she realised she was in a very exposed position indeed.

Instinct told her to find somewhere to hide at once, but what good would that do? She was stranded with no money, no car, and virtually no clothes. Her only hope was to get to the rendezvous point. So, steeling herself, the near-naked beauty set off determinedly in the direction of the village.

For the next five minutes or so she walked alone. There were neither cars nor pedestrians on the quiet road, and she made good progress. Gradually she began to regain her confidence - but then she heard the sound of approaching motorcycles.

Instantly her fears returned in a rush of adrenaline, and she began to search frantically for some kind of cover. The hedge and fence on both sides were unbroken, offering no hope at all, and she gave a despairing cry as the sound of the machines grew louder. Then she saw a telegraph pole set hard alongside the fence. It wasn't much, she knew, but there was nothing else. Behind her she could already see the glow of the headlights in the sky, and she knew she had no time to think. She hurried towards the pole, the frightening roar of the machines filling her head.

Reaching the pole, gasping with exertion and distress, she pressed herself between it and the fence, and no sooner had she done so than the road was illuminated by powerful headlights. She tried to mould herself back against the rough wood, watching them as they passed. There were six machines, each one loud and powerful, the throbbing engines filling the night with their roar. She prayed that none of the riders would look back and see her pale figure pinned to the pole, and sighed with relief as the last of the red tail-lights disappeared round a bend from view. Still she remained where she was, waiting for the beat of her heart to slow and her breathing to return to normal, and by the time she emerged the night was as silent as it had been before.

Laura stood in the road, momentarily reluctant to leave the meagre shelter she had discovered. It had been an unnerving experience, yet at the same time it had been extraordinarily exciting. Something about the rough, masculine men on their heavy machines had appealed to her most perverse desires and, as she slipped a hand down and ran it over the thin gusset of her pants, she was shocked at the wetness she found there.

She walked on, thoroughly aroused now, her hands straying up to caress her firm breasts through the thin material or to gently rub her erect clitoris, sending pulses of excitement through her slim frame as she went. As she made her way along the empty lane she was unable to free her mind of erotic images of the bikers. She imagined them surrounding her, reaching out to feel her flesh, heedless of her protests. She saw them becoming more confident as they recognised her submissiveness, ripping off her skimpy garments and groping her. Then they were dragging her down to her knees and ramming their thick cocks into her mouth as they held her, just like the hunters had done with Belita. As these vivid images filled her fertile imagination, it was all Laura could do not to stop right there and masturbate in the middle of the road.

She turned a corner, and then halted, the perils of her present predicament suddenly pushing the fantasies from her mind. Ahead of her she could see the glow of a streetlamp, and she knew she was approaching the village. Once again icy fingers of apprehension gripped her as she was reminded of her situation. She thought carefully of what she had seen when they passed through in Cassandra's car. There had been nobody about, the curtains of the houses drawn, the shops closed. Only one building had been lit, and that she had glimpsed briefly as they passed. Perhaps she had nothing to fear.

But still her footsteps began to falter as she approached the streetlight. She knew that anyone seeing her beneath its apron of light would see at once how little she wore. But she walked on, moving further into the village, passing beneath another streetlight, then another, her nipples hardening as she contemplated how exposed she was. To her right she spotted the building she had glimpsed earlier with lights on inside. It was set back a little down a lane, and now a van was parked in front of it. Laura paused briefly by the side road, watching and listening; there didn't seem to be anyone around, so she moved on.

She was reaching the centre of the village now, so if escape became a necessity she would have to flee as far in either direction. Then something up ahead caught her eye, and she froze.

There were people there; vague figures standing beside the road. She narrowed her eyes, trying to make them out. On either side of the street were terraced cottages, so staying close to their walls she edged forward, still trying to make out the people in the road, peering into the semi-darkness... and then

Laura knew exactly what she was seeing.

It was the bikers. They had stopped their machines by a bus shelter and were milling around them, talking and drinking from bottles and cans.

Laura groaned with dismay. There was absolutely no way she could get past the group without being seen. And heaven knew what they would do if they saw her. Suddenly her fantasies became all too real, and she pressed herself further back against the wall.

She watched them. They seemed to be settled where they were, and showed no sign of wanting to move. To her right was a church tower with a clock, and she glanced at the time. Ten thirty-five. Time was running out. If she didn't find a way past them soon, she'd really be in trouble.

If only there was a back lane she could use. But the only way through the village seemed to be just the one main street. Then she thought back to where she had seen the van down the side street. Perhaps that would offer her an opportunity to find a way around the bikers. She glanced back, reluctant to retreat, but it seemed to be the only chance she had. Slowly she turned and began to retrace her steps.

She reached the lane and peered down it, and thankfully there was no sign of life. Cautiously, she began to make her way towards the van, and as she got closer she saw there was a second one parked beyond it. The lights from the building beside them were still on, and then she saw a movement from within, and realised it was a small grotty cafe.

She moved on, staying in the shadows and away from the building as much as possible. Then, just as she thought things were beginning to go her way, she stopped abruptly and cursed under her breath; the lane was a dead-end, blocked off by a high wall.

'Hey, what are you doing?'

Laura squealed with dismay and spun round to face a man standing beside the first van, holding a grubby road atlas. He was trying to peer at her through the dark shadows. 'Why you lurking around there?' he demanded.

Laura's heart began to pound as she realised she was trapped, with the dead-end behind her and the man in front. As she stood there, wondering what on earth to do, the man slammed the van door shut and moved closer.

'What are you doing there?' he demanded again. He was sturdy and squat, with stout tattooed forearms and a thick mat of hair sprouting from a checked shirt, which was unbuttoned down to the swell of a large belly that rolled over the waistband of his ragged jeans. Instinctively Laura tried in vain to cover herself with her hands.

'I - I was just out walking,' she stammered unconvincingly.

'What, dressed like that?' he snorted.

'It was kind of a dare,' she added. 'A forfeit.'

'You what?'

'A forfeit. I lost a game, so I had to go out like this.'

He moved closer and studied her with a lick of his lips. 'So, where are you going?' he asked gruffly.

It was hopeless; she might as well tell the truth. 'I'm going to the pub on the edge of the village,' she said, pointing in the vague direction. 'I have to meet someone there.'

'So, what are you doing down here?'

'There are some bikers on the road,' she told him. 'I can't get past them like this.'

He shook his head. 'I've seen some strange things in my time,' he sniggered, 'but you beat all. Come on into the cafe.'

'B-but I can't,' she protested. 'Not like this.' But he grabbed her, his brawny fingers easily encompassing her upper arm.

'Come on,' he ordered.

Laura protested again, but her words fell on deaf ears. He was like a bulldog, and when he shoved her towards the cafe she had little choice but to go.

As they reached the door he pulled it open and thrust her inside. Laura staggered to a halt on the threshold, an arm wrapped across her breasts and a hand covering the front of her panties.

There were two men in the cafe. One sat at a table, a mug of steaming tea in front of him, and his eyebrows lifted as he saw the young beauty in her scanty underwear.

The second man was standing behind the counter with the stub of a rolled cigarette stuck between his lips, idly rubbing a tea mug with a greasy tea cloth, and wearing an even greasier apron. 'What's going on, Doug?' he asked. 'Who's she?'

'Caught her skulking about outside.'

'What is she, a whore looking for business?' sneered the other driver. 'She won't find much around here, will she?'

The man called Doug nudged Laura in the ribs. 'Tell them what you told me.'

Laura, her face scarlet, stammered out her explanation, watching the expressions of amusement on the men's faces.

'So basically you're saying you've got no clothes and you've to get to some woman before she goes home?' the man behind the counter chuckled. 'Shit, you must be dumb.'

Laura hung her head abjectly; after all, he was right.

'What do you think, Les?' Doug asked the driver sipping his tea.

'I think she's gonna need our help. There's no way she'll get past those bikers like that, and on her own.'

'Can you help?' Laura asked hopefully, brightening a little.

'That depends,' he said thoughtfully. 'After all, you got yourself into this. No decent girl would go about dressed like that, would she?'

'I... I suppose not,' she admitted.

'Let Les and Frank here see exactly what you're wearing,' Doug prompted, nudging her in the back to emphasise his order.

Laura looked at him in alarm. 'Please, I...'

54

'Show them!' he barked, and then grinned when she visibly flinched away from his aggression.

Laura looked at the three men in turn. What choice did she have? They said they could help her. Surely she was safer with them than with a gang of rowdy bikers? So slowly, her cheeks glowing, she allowed her hands to fall to her sides.

Les gave a low whistle, and Laura stared at the dirty tiled floor as she felt his eyes crawl all over her body. 'Shit,' he breathed, 'if you were my daughter I'd put you over my knee.'

'I reckon somebody's already done that,' said Doug. 'Turn round and show them.'

Laura's heart plummeted even further; the marks of her chastisement were still evident, and could be seen through the gossamer red underwear.

'Go on, show them,' insisted Doug.

Slowly the mortified youngster turned.

'Shit, someone's given her a good thrashing, and no mistake,' said Frank. 'You like having your arse thrashed, darlin'?'

Laura said nothing, but closed her eyes, wondering when her nightmare would end.

'Anyway,' said Doug. 'Our lovely little exhibitionist here has a problem and she wants us to help her, don't you, love?'

Laura nodded silently.

'Well, I reckon I could get you to the *Red Dragon* in two or three minutes. And you have to be there by eleven fifteen, you say?'

She nodded again, feeling a little more hopeful.

He glanced at his watch and grinned broadly. 'Good, that gives us about twenty-five minutes. Just time for you to earn your ride.'

'What do you mean, earn?' she asked, although she really did not have to.

'We just want you to do as you're told for a little while. Then, if we're pleased with you, I'll drive you where you want to go.'

'And what do I have to do?' Again, it was a pointless question.

'First of all,' Doug went on, warming to his task, 'give your underwear to Frank, there. They'll make great trophies on the wall.'

'But, they're all I've got on,' she protested.

'That's right,' he said smugly. 'Come on, we already know you're not a shy girl.'

Although Laura hated to finally accept the severity of her predicament, it was clear that she wouldn't get away without surrendering to the three of them, so with shaking hands she reached for the clip that held her bra closed at the front. Then, taking a deep breath, she snapped it open.

The skimpy cups popped apart and Laura's firm succulent breasts thrust fully into view, the dark nipples rigid and proud. Three grunts told her the ogling men approved, and then Frank moved from behind the counter and held out a hand. Blushing intensely, Laura handed him the bra.

'And the rest,' Doug demanded.

The panties were lowered and she gracefully stepped out of them, leaving her naked apart from her shoes. Once again Frank reached for the tiny scrap of silk and she handed it to him.

Laura stood before the three lechers, feeling utterly vulnerable. Why oh why was she so foolish to get into such awful situations?

Doug was the first to move, possessively wrapping a tree-like arm around her trim waist, virtually engulfing it. Laura dared not move, standing rigid as he molested her, cupping a breast in his shovel of a hand, and all the time Frank and Les stared, watching her face for any reactions.

Then she felt his other hand sliding down her flank, then moving round to the front, and she gasped disgracefully as his fingers found her clitoris, sending a spasm of sheer lustful pleasure through her pinned frame.

'You like that, you little tart, don't you?' he murmured in her ear, loud enough for his accomplices to hear.

'Mmmm...' Laura couldn't help but relax back against him, all thoughts of resistance slipping from her mind as the pleasure became too much for her to resist. Doug clearly sensed her surrender, his fingers tracing the length of her wet sex as he exchanged knowing looks with the other two.

'She's wet as hell,' he grunted with satisfaction.

The other two leered and nodded. Frank placed her underwear on the nearest table and, as she watched through misty eyes, he tucked his dirty apron into his belt, unzipped his fly and brusquely tugged out his meaty cock. 'You fancy tasting some of this, little slut?' he jeered.

She gazed at him, barely able to believe how the night was unravelling. 'I...'

'Of course you do,' Doug hissed into her ear, giving her a little shake that made her squeal. 'You wouldn't be walking the streets with fuck all on if you weren't a little cocksucker. Now chew Frank's cock for him.' He pushed her forward and down onto he knees.

Laura looked up at the man looming over her. His apron was streaked with grease and food stains, his paunch hung over his belt and he was unshaven, his face shiny with sweat. But she had no option. She was alone and naked with three randy brutes, and she must do as they ordered if she was to get back to Cassandra safely. Her eyes dropped to his stiff penis as it jutted aggressively from his shabby trousers.

With trembling fingers she reached up and lightly curled them around his shaft, feeling the way it throbbed beneath them. She ran them along its length, tracing the turgid vein that ran down its underside. Then she gingerly leaned forward and, peeling apart her moist lips, pursed them about the bulbous glans and began to suck.

Frank wheezed. 'That's right, baby,' he croaked. 'Suck it hard. Go on.'

He pressed his hips forward, forcing himself deeper into Laura's mouth. Suppressing her natural desire to gag, she responded by sucking harder, her tongue licking the gnarled flesh as she did, her hands against his thighs in an instinctive but futile gesture to stop him pushing too deep.

The man's excitement increased, and her shame was forgotten as she became more and more infected by his arousal. And the more she sucked, the more her body responded to his taste and scent. She was like some animal on heat, her gorgeous body tingling with arousal, her carnal instincts taking over from her logical mind as her wanton nature swept to the fore.

She was aware of the eyes of his cohorts crawling all over her, and of the remarks they were making about her, but she didn't care any more. All that mattered was Frank's orgasm.

And he came with a grunt and an extra lunge of his hips, her mouth filling with sperm, his erection pulsing between her lips as he pumped his seed into her throat. She remained still, on her knees, her eyes closed as she obediently swallowed, her lips sealed around the root of his shaft until his jerky movements finally stopped. Then she slowly eased back onto her heels, the softening flesh plopping from between her lips and bobbing against her chin, and gazed up at him with innocent eyes.

'Shit, she's good,' he murmured, tucking his dormant penis back into his pants. 'Best blowjob I've had in ages.'

'Let's see what she fucks like, then,' Les suggested. 'Get her over the table, guys.'

Doug and Frank hauled her to her feet. Ignoring her half-hearted protests they dragged her across the nearest table. It was covered with a blue and white checked plastic tablecloth, which was splattered with food and drink stains from previous occupants, but the men simply threw her forward, scattering the condiments as her slim form was pressed downwards. The surface felt cool and hard against Laura's breasts, tummy and hips.

Doug held her down on one side, Frank on the other, so that she was powerless to move. Then she felt Les's hands pressing her thighs apart. She strained round to see him looming behind her, staring down at the smooth curve of her back, at the firm globes of her bottom and at her sex and anus, both of which were exposed to his view. Deeply ashamed, Laura struggled to find a more modest position, but the men were too strong for her, their muscular hands gripping her arms and legs and holding her where she lay.

She heard the sound of a zipper being pulled down and glanced back again. Len had released his cock and it jutted from his jeans, the foreskin stretched back in readiness of the delights to come. There was a drop of moisture on the tip and, as he rubbed his foreskin back and forth in his fist, it spread across the shiny surface of his glans.

The sight of his weapon sent a new shudder of excitement through Laura's pinned frame. Being restrained thus, naked and helpless, was rekindling her memories of Belita and the way the hunters had used her, and once again her perverse desires were aroused by the rough attitude of the three men. She was theirs for the taking whether she liked it or not, and her own needs or desires were of no interest to them as they took their pleasure in her.

She moaned as she felt the bulbous tip of Len's erection probe between her thighs, and as it did her sex convulsed, anointing the intruder with her juices.

'Hell, she's hot for it,' he gloated.

'Go on, Len,' urged Doug. 'Give the slut what she wants,' and then a low moan escaped Laura's lips as she felt him push his cock up between her thighs and press it against her sex lips. It slipped in easily and he sank home, bringing a wail of pleasure from the young beauty as she revelled in the sensation of having a cock inside her once again. He continued to press until his throbbing organ filled her, and then he began to fuck her.

It was a hard, vigorous fucking, with no thought given for Laura's comfort or enjoyment as the randy driver rutted against her. Every thrust of his hips forced her against the hard edge of the table, making it dig painfully into her as he forced the air from her lungs.

Yet despite the discomfort, the filthy table, the hands gripping her arms and thighs, and the humiliation, Laura was more turned on than ever, her succulent channel contracting around the thick rod that invaded her as if trying to draw it still deeper.

A hand grasped her hair, pulling her head roughly round, and she saw that Doug had discarded his jeans and pants, his own erection spearing from beneath his shirt. Once again there was no thought for Laura's comfort as he dragged her closer and nudged his cock against her mouth. She parted her lips and, for the second time in only a few minutes, found herself sucking a rock hard erection, the smell and taste of male arousal filling her senses as her shapely body was shunted by the man behind her, between her parted thighs.

For Laura it was all too much. The exposure in her sexy underwear, the humility of the men's treatment of her, the taste and feel of her double penetration in the seedy little cafe suddenly combined into a spasm of excitement that sent her over the top. She came with a groan, her hips grinding against the table as the glorious pleasure of an orgasm overcame her. She cried aloud, the sound muffled by her mouthful of male erection as she succumbed to her desires, even the sound of the men's laughter at her wantonness not able to dampen her ardour.

She was still at the peak of her climax when she felt the first spurt of semen shoot deep into her vagina. She groaned with pleasure as she felt him release his load into her, his cock seeming to thicken still more as jet after jet of thick fluid flooded her womb. She was almost out of control, writhing about in ecstasy as she accepted his seed inside her, oblivious to the fact that the uncouth men were treating her as little more than a sex vessel, and actually revelling in their rough treatment.

No sooner had Len pulled from her than the erection in her mouth was withdrawn and she felt herself being lifted and turned onto her back. They lay her across the table once more, stretching her legs apart and dragging her forward so that the edge dug into the tender flesh of her bottom. She gazed wearily up at Doug, who stood between her thighs, his stiff rod glistening with her saliva. Then she moaned anew as he thrust into her with one powerful lunge, grasping her thighs and pulling her forward as he buried his pulsating weapon to the hilt.

Once again it was a rough coupling. He continually butted his groin against her, making her breasts tremor deliciously with every stroke. Laura simply lay back and let him take her, all fight draining away as she abandoned herself to them, another orgasm approaching.

He was pumping harder now, beads of sweat coating his forehead, avid concentration etched on his face, his breathing laboured. His companions were no longer holding her, having sensed her surrender, and they stood on either side of the creaking table leering down at her.

Doug came suddenly, a hoarse grunt escaping his throat as he shot his load into the beautiful girl, and the sensation of the hot fluid flooding her was the final trigger for Laura. Her whimpers echoed around the grimy place as another delicious orgasm shook her curvaceous frame, her back arched up from the table, her breasts quivering as she lost herself in carnal passion.

He continued to hold her, grinding his cock as she writhed on the unsteady table, her rambling cries abating as fatigue finally caused her pleasures to ebb. He went on rutting, slowing gradually until he was totally spent, then pulled out, leaving Laura slumped across the table, her breasts rising and falling as she regained her breath.

He grinned at the other two. 'At least the service in this place is getting better,' he sniggered.

Chapter 13

Laura said nothing as the van pulled out from the dark car park and turned onto the main village street. Doug sat in the driver's seat, a contented grin on his face as he drove, occasionally glancing across at his lovely companion.

She was still naked, apart from her shoes. As he had threatened, Frank kept her underwear, hanging it up on hooks behind the counter like a hunter's trophies. Laura wondered how many men would stop there in the future and would see the evidence of her debauched visit. She imagined Frank telling the story, and of the jealous faces of the drivers who had not been there to witness the beautiful youngster who had walked into the establishment wearing next-to-nothing and who had given herself so freely to those inside.

Laura's hand stole down to her sex. They had allowed her to quickly wash in the decidedly unhygienic toilet after finishing with her, and she shivered slightly as her fingers brushed against her clitoris and she recalled how aroused the men had made her.

The van's headlights picked out the motorcycles still parked at the side of the road. The bikers were still hovering around them, still drinking heavily and looking a lot more rowdy than before. They were a rough looking crowd, she mused, about seven in all, wearing tattered and oily denims.

'These the guys you were trying to avoid?' asked Doug as they drew closer.

Lisa nodded.

'Well, I guess their loss was our gain,' he said, chuckling lecherously.

They nearly didn't make it. As they approached the pub Laura could see the headlights of a car moving across the car park, and Doug pulled his van across the entrance as Cassandra's car reached it.

He turned to Laura. 'This is where you get out,' he said. 'Any time you want to come back to visit us you're *more* than welcome.'

Laura climbed quickly from the cab; more people might be leaving the pub and she was anxious not to be seen. As the van pulled away she dashed round to the passenger door of the car, and Cassandra watched without expression as she climbed in and slammed it behind her.

'What happened to your underwear?' she asked.

'I lost it,' Laura snapped bluntly. 'Let's go, shall we?'

'Who was that guy?'

'Just a van driver. Come on, there's people over there. They might have seen me.'

'Are you going to tell me everything that happened this evening?'

Laura said nothing, but stared straight ahead indignantly.

'I want to know every detail,' Cassandra warned, and then she eased the car out onto the dark country road.

Chapter 14

Laura stared across at the mirror opposite her, her eyes fixed on her own reflection, unable to tear her gaze from what she saw.

She was naked, as she had been since arriving back at the house with Cassandra. She glanced down at her breasts, wincing slightly as the clamps that were attached to her nipples glinted in the light of the bare room.

Her gaze dropped to her thighs. Sitting as she was, with her ankles bound to the chair legs and her knees pulled apart by straps attached to the chair arms at the sides, her sex was exposed and vulnerable.

Experimentally she twisted her arms behind her back, trying desperately to pull them from the tight leather straps that ensnared her wrists and held them firmly to the back of the chair. She struggled in vain, though. Cassandra had done a thorough job, and she was held securely with nothing to do but ponder her weary reflection.

Her mind went back over the events of the evening. How had she ever allowed herself to be left alone in a strange place wearing nothing but the most revealing underwear? The outcome had been inevitable, surely? It was simply a case of who would find her first. She strained round and looked over her shoulder at the door. It was firmly closed, and bolted from the outside. She still didn't understand quite what was going on, having expected Cassandra to allow her to shower and go straight to bed after her ordeal. But instead the woman had taken her straight to the small outhouse at the back of the main one, where the instruments of her bondage were waiting. At first she protested, but knew deep down that she was no match for the domineering housekeeper, so she submitted meekly, suppressing her feelings of humiliation as she was made helpless once more.

The nipple clamps were the worst of it. It was not until she was tightly trussed, her arms trapped behind her so that her breasts thrust provocatively forward, that Cassandra had produced them. First, though, she caressed Laura's breasts, stroking and squeezing her nipples until, much to Laura's shame, they stood proudly erect. Only then did she snap the jaws over the turgid teats. The torturous caresses had intensified their sensitivity, and Laura bit her lip to suppress a whimper as the cruel teeth sank into her flesh.

Laura had not known what to expect next, but when Cassandra produced a black dildo she could not, to her secret shame, suppress a delightful shiver of anticipation. But taking Laura completely by surprise, Cassandra fed it into her mouth, making her suck it, the smell and bitter taste of the rubber somehow exciting the bound girl still further. Then she teased her with it, pressing it between her thighs and against her sex lips, which pouted and moistened. But then, just as the confused girl was pressing her hips forward against it, Cassandra withdrew and hung it on the side of the mirror, where it was now, as if to taunt the naked, aroused beauty.

For the next half hour or so Laura was made to recount her story, revealing every detail of her encounter with the three rough men. Cassandra made her describe every moment, eliciting details of precisely how she had felt, making her describe the intensity of her orgasms.

Despite her mortal shame at what she had done, Laura found herself becoming more and more aroused as she relived her sordid ravishment at the hands of the three strangers. Every now and again Cassandra would take down the dildo and tease her with it, rubbing it lightly over her swollen clitoris and smiling wolfishly. She did no more than tease though, making the girl wail pitifully with the frustration of an orgasm, so close yet unattainable, as she hung the dildo back in full view of her.

Then, when Laura came to the end of her tale, Cassandra did something she did not expect. She left her alone. Pausing only to kiss her, the housekeeper left and locked the door, leaving her captive alone to contemplate her own perversities as she studied her shameful reflection in the mirror.

Laura thought she had heard the car start, but couldn't be sure. Then there was nothing but the silence of the room and the turmoil of her thoughts as she struggled to keep her arousal at bay.

She wasn't sure how long ago Cassandra had left. An hour at least, possibly two. Eventually, despite the pain and discomfort of her bondage, she began to doze off, only to find herself dreaming the most erotic of dreams, in which she was pursued by men with enormous erections who ravished her mercilessly.

And then she was wide-awake once more. A sound had roused her, although she wasn't sure what. Then she heard it again, and realised it was the sound of the door bolts being slowly drawn back. She looked fearfully at the handle as it turned. What if Cassandra wasn't alone? What if she had brought somebody back with her to share Laura's shame? She knew the woman was capable of such a thing, and felt the blood rush to her cheeks as she thought of the sight she made, completely naked, her legs spread wide and her breasts thrust forward, her nipples clamped.

But to her relief Cassandra was alone, and she closed the door and smiled at the confused and timid face of her captive.

'Cassandra, where have you been?' she asked cautiously. 'What have...?'

Cassandra placed a manicured finger to Laura's lips. 'Hush, my little wanton,' she said, a smile in her eyes but not on her lips. She ran her other hand down Laura's flat tummy, stroking through her soft pubic hair then gently finding and rubbing her clitoris, inducing a sweet gasp from the bound girl.

'Still wet, I see,' she said pensively, holding up a glistening finger for Laura to see. She wiped it across the upper slopes of Laura's breasts, leaving a silvery streak on the soft flesh.

'What's going on, Cassandra?' Laura pleaded meekly. 'Where did you go?'

'Just to talk with some people,' the woman mused. 'Now, my little beauty, let me tell you of my plans.'

'What plans? Haven't I done enough?'

Cassandra smiled again. 'There is so much more to come, my sweet,' she purred cryptically. 'So many more experiences for a girl as licentious as yourself.'

'But I... I think I've gone far enough already, don't you?'

Cassandra stroked Laura's hair, a thoughtful expression on her face. 'Yes, you've come a long way,' she agreed. 'But there's still much more.'

'More?'

'Well, think about it. You've experienced a great deal in the last few weeks, and all of it has simply made you want to experience more.'

'No...'

'Believe me,' Cassandra went on, 'I know. Even these dear nipple clamps are giving you a thrill, I can tell.'

Laura did not answer, her eyes dropping to the silver jewellery that decorated her breasts. Cassandra was, as usual and infuriatingly, correct. The new instruments of torture, excruciating though they were, were adding a dimension to her arousal that she had barely dreamt possible, and as the woman tugged them the gasp that escaped her lips was more one of pleasure than pain.

'So what do you say, my sweet?' Cassandra went on. 'Are you game for the ultimate?'

Laura shuddered. 'Wh-what are you suggesting?' she whispered.

'That you give yourself completely, as a slave.'

'I don't understand.'

'Oh, I think you do,' Cassandra smiled. 'That you give yourself to those who will treat you with disdain. Who will humiliate you and use you like you've never been used before.'

Laura stared at the woman, her stomach churning as she heard the words and absorbed their meaning. Surely she couldn't be expected to degrade herself any more than she had done already? 'I can't do any more,' she stated determinedly. 'Haven't you had enough from me?'

The housekeeper shook her head. 'No, Laura,' she said. 'We must take this next vital step. We must continue your training.'

Laura shook her head. 'I won't do it,' she said. 'This has gone far enough, Cassandra. Now please let me go.'

Cassandra laughed. It was not a pleasant laugh; its tone was mocking, and there was a confidence in her expression that told the helpless girl that her pleas were falling on deaf ears. 'I think you'll change your mind when you see this, my precious little slut,' she said.

She moved to the mirror and pushed it aside, and behind it, to Laura's surprise, stood a television mounted on a trolley, with a video recorder underneath. 'Now, we're going to watch a little show, my pretty one,' she said. 'Won't that be nice?'

With a sinking feeling Laura watched as the woman switched it on, produced a tape, and popped it into the recorder. Then she stood back.

For a few moments fuzzy snow filled the screen. Then it stopped, and Laura found herself staring at a dark, barely discernible image. For a few seconds she could make out nothing - then she realised she was looking at a quiet street at night. As she watched a figure emerged from the shadows.

'Oh, no...' she gasped, shaking her head in denial as the figure moved furtively closer. It was her in the scanty red underwear, creeping through the village mere hours before. 'I... I don't understand,' whispered the dismayed girl, her eyes glued to the silent screen.

'You didn't think I'd miss the show, surely?' the woman ridiculed. 'A conveniently parked van was all I needed. But keep watching - it gets better.'

The picture changed. This time it was the lane where the diner was. A familiar figure was creeping towards it, trying hard to conceal itself in the shadows. Laura watched in horrified fascination as another figure, stout and holding a roadmap, climbed out of one of the vans and confronted her.

The tape rolled on. Cassandra had moved close to the diner windows once the trucker and his reluctant companion had disappeared inside, and captured the whole sordid performance.

'Turn it off...' Laura pleaded quietly, still watching the disgraceful show. 'Please turn it off.' But her pleading had no effect on Cassandra, a smile playing about her lips as the girl on the screen dropped her bra, revealing her breasts to the drooling men. Moments later her panties followed, and she stood naked.

For the next fifteen minutes Laura was forced to witness her debauched experience and behaviour, and worst of all, her own enjoyment was unmistakable.

It was the most humiliating experience of Laura's life, to be forced to sit and watch as she gave herself shamelessly to the randy men. She wished she had put up some kind of resistance, or at least managed to keep her own reprehensible yearnings in check.

Yet, despite her mortification at what she was witnessing, Laura couldn't suppress the desires the images were stirring up. The more she watched the more she wanted to feel the real thing once more, and by the time the screen finally went blank she was trembling with longing.

Cassandra switched off the television. 'Well, pretty little slut,' she said, 'what do you think of that?'

'You had no right,' Laura said defiantly, lifting her chin.

'Nevertheless, I have the tape,' Cassandra pointed out. 'I wonder how your guardian will respond when he sees it?'

Laura let out a cry of dismay. 'No!' she wailed. 'You can't show it to *him*!'

'Oh, but I think you'll find I can - and I will,' Cassandra gloated. 'Unless...'

'Unless what?'

'Unless you reconsider what I said earlier.'

Laura stared at the woman, scarcely able to believe her ears. So that was it - she was being blackmailed. 'B-but why?' she gasped.

'Never mind why. Let's just say that your antics give me pleasure.'

'Look,' said Laura, desperation creeping into her voice. 'Why don't we just do something together again? I'll do whatever you say - whatever you want... I'll do anything to please you.'

Cassandra stroked the girl's smooth cheek. 'I know you will,' she said confidently. 'And shall I tell you what you are going to do?'

Laura gazed up into the woman's eyes, then her gaze dropped. 'Please...' she said lamely.

Cassandra moved to the mirror and unhooked the black dildo. She ran her fingers along its length, tracing the undulations on its surface with her fingers while staring down at her naked captive. Laura tried to hide her emotions as he eyed the dildo, but knew that the shiver of excitement that ran through her body had not gone unnoticed by the woman.

'Watching yourself has made you feel sexy again, hasn't it?' she stated, caressing the phallus with the reverence of a collector holding a priceless artefact. 'Do you want me to use this on you?'

Laura said nothing and lowered her eyes in a futile attempt to conceal her guilt; had she been alone, in the privacy of her bedroom, she would have used the dildo on herself - and she knew the manipulative woman knew it too.

Cassandra reached down and unclipped one of the nipple clamps. At once a new surge of pain filled the hapless captive as the blood rushed back into her tender teat. Cassandra removed the second clamp, bringing more agony to the helpless girl, her nipples throbbing, the small teeth leaving their mark.

Cassandra caressed Laura's breasts, kneading the silky flesh with her fingers. 'Shall I tell you what's going to happen?' she asked.

Laura remained silent, but Cassandra went on anyway.

'In a few day's time your guardian and his good lady wife go away on holiday,' she announced. 'Naturally he'll be expecting you to join them in the south of France, but unfortunately you won't be able to.'

'Why?' Laura could not withhold the question.

'Because you're going down with the 'flu just before they leave, and fortunately for you, Sir John's housekeeper...' she smiled broadly and added unnecessarily '...that's me - is staying here while they're away, and she will volunteer to look after you.'

'But what if I don't co-operate?' Laura countered with more defiance than she really felt.

'But you will co-operate, won't you my dear?' As she spoke, Cassandra slid the tip of the dildo down over Laura's belly and moved it between her legs, and Laura gasped as she felt it press against her tender clitoris.

'Wh-what then?' she asked, trying to ignore the delicious sensations the rubber object was bringing her.

'Then you'll be going on your own little holiday. A walking holiday.'

Laura frowned and shook her head. 'No, I still don't understand.'

'I'll be taking you to a place a fair distance away from here. Then I'll be leaving you on your own. Who knows, you might just have a few days to yourself. I don't think so, though.'

'Then what's going to happen - oh...' Laura gave a sigh as Cassandra slid the phallus into her vagina. So wet was she that it slipped in easily, forcing its way deep into the heat and wetness of her sex. 'Please, don't,' she moaned hopelessly.

'Oh yes,' Cassandra cooed, watching the girl closely. 'You'll be all alone. Just like Belita in the story. And you remember what happened to Belita, don't you?'

'Mmmm.' The image of Belita sent a new surge of lust washing through the defenceless girl.

'That's got you excited, little slut,' smiled Cassandra. She began working the dildo back and forth, drawing fresh moans of desire from the writhing nubile. 'As I said,' she went on, 'you may be left alone, but I think not. If they catch you they'll show no mercy. They'll use this pretty body of yours just as I'm doing. They'll do whatever they want with you. And there will be no escape. You'll be their slave.'

As she spoke, Laura came, a flow of sheer wanton pleasure sweeping through her as her body finally succumbed to the depraved desires within. She shuddered, her breasts quivering deliciously as she abandoned herself to the thick dildo that was pumping back and forth inside her.

The orgasm went on and on, with Laura's plaintive cries echoing around the tiny room as her lust took complete control. Cassandra continued to work the rubber column back and forth until Laura was drained, her sweat-covered body heaving as she fought to retain her breath. Then, leaving the dildo embedded inside her panting captive, Cassandra eased back and scrutinised her with satisfaction in her eyes.

'That's right, little one,' she said, 'enjoy. And next week you're going to have the most exciting adventure of your life.'

Chapter 15

Laura lay in bed, listening to the sounds in the house below, feeling restless, the blankets tucked up around her. On her bedside cabinet were a glass of water and a bottle of cough syrup. The curtains were drawn, so that the room was bathed in a pale light.

She looked at the clock; her guardian must leave soon if they were to catch their flight to France. She wondered if he would look in before he left, but knew it was unlikely. She had never known him to enter her bedroom in all the time she'd lived there, and she hoped fervently that he wouldn't break that habit today. She certainly didn't want him to see her.

She had begun the charade of her illness the previous afternoon, complaining of hot flushes and feeling weak. Soon afterwards she retired to her room, feeling horribly uncomfortable with the deception, all the more so because of Cassandra's presence. The woman had treated her as if she were genuinely unwell, ensuring that her meals were brought to her room, and reporting back to her guardian about her condition.

'I have told Sir John that you will be in no state to fly tomorrow,' she had said to Laura. 'And he agrees that you should remain here in my care.'

Laura had not responded, unwilling to enter the conspiracy with the woman, although she knew that she was already guilty of deceit, and now she knew it was her last chance to tell the truth and face the consequences of Sir John's wrath.

For a moment she was tempted to throw herself at his mercy, to reveal all and save herself from the diabolical plan Cassandra had in store for her. But, even as the idea crossed her mind, she knew she couldn't go through with it. No matter how much she dreaded the humiliation that was to come, dread of her guardian's wrath was equally daunting. So it was with a heavy heart that she lay in her bedroom, listening to the car drive away.

No more than ten minutes had passed before the anxious girl heard the tread of the housekeeper on the stairs. The rest of the staff, she knew, had been granted leave, and she was now alone in the house with the woman who exercised such power over her.

The door opened and Cassandra came in, wearing a crisp white blouse and neat black skirt. She was holding a plastic carrier bag, and placed it on the bed beside Laura.

'Come on, little one,' she purred. 'Time to stop this charade and get changed.'

'Listen, Cassandra,' Laura said, desperately hoping to reason with her, 'can't we just forget all this? I mean, you've got your way; I'm here with you alone. Couldn't you just do what you want with me here? I won't complain. I'll do anything you tell me to.'

Cassandra shook her head. 'Oh no,' she said. 'What I have in mind for you goes way beyond that. Now get up and put this on; we have to be leaving soon.' She held the bag for Laura, who accepted it tentatively and peered inside. It contained a short black dress and a pair of leather sandals. She pulled them out and searched for underwear - but there was none.

'Just put on what's in the bag,' Cassandra snapped, reading Laura's misgivings. 'Hurry up now, or I'll get impatient.'

Laura slipped slowly from between the sheets. She looked at Cassandra, wondering if she was to be allowed any privacy, but the housekeeper made no move, so she turned away and reluctantly reached for the hem of her nightgown and pulled it off over her head. Then she fumbled with the dress, anxious to cover her nudity, already feeling the colour rising in her cheeks.

The dress was a simple one, with buttons up the front. It had no sleeves, and the plunging neckline and tight bodice showed off Laura's deep cleavage and exquisitely shaped breasts to perfection. It was a snug fit, moulding to her curves as she did up the buttons, the hem tight about the tops of her shapely thighs. She slipped her feet into the sandals.

'Come here,' demanded Cassandra, and Laura turned to the woman. 'Mmm, very nice,' she said approvingly. 'Come on now, let's get going.'

The beautiful girl followed the older woman out of the room and along the landing. They descended the stairs, with Laura agitatedly checking the hem of the short dress as it threatened with every step to ride up. When they reached the front door she hesitated, dreading the prospect of her coming ordeal.

Cassandra's car was parked in the driveway, and she walked across and opened the door before turning back to Laura, who was still hovering at the entrance. 'Come on, Laura,' she said impatiently. 'Get in the car.'

Taking a final guilty glance around, Laura made her way to the car as quickly as she could, and as she slid into the passenger seat the dress rode up, exposing her shadowy pubic mound. Placing her hands in her lap and clamping her thighs tightly together she sat, staring straight ahead, her cheeks glowing.

Cassandra slipped effortlessly in beside her and started the engine, and as they swept out of the long driveway Laura stole a wistful glance back at the house. Never had she thought she would be reluctant to leave the place, but with the dread of what was to come, she would have given anything to stay there and hide.

They drove in silence along roads that were completely unfamiliar to Laura. It was nearly an hour before Cassandra slowed the car, then turned down a narrow track between overhanging trees. They came to a halt before a tall gate set in an equally tall metal fence. Hanging on the gate was a sign:

Private Property. Keep Out.

Cassandra cut the engine, and then turned to Laura. 'This is the place,' she said.

Laura did not like the look of things at all. 'B-but, there's nothing here,' she blurted.

'Would you prefer to be left in the middle of town?' Cassandra countered sarcastically.

Laura shook her head solemnly.

They got out of the car and Cassandra produced a key from her pocket and went to the gate. It was secured with a padlock and chain, which she removed, pushing it open. Beyond was a track that disappeared into a dense wood, and judging from the foreboding gate and fence and the warning sign, it was all ominously private.

Cassandra stood aside. Laura stepped through the entrance, and then stopped. 'I still don't understand,' she complained. 'Where am I going?'

'There's an old manor house about a mile from here,' Cassandra explained, somewhat vaguely.

'So, you're just leaving me here?'

'That's right.'

'But I thought...' Laura's voice trailed away. This wasn't what she had expected at all. She had expected to be delivered directly into the hands of some lecherous brutes, but it now seemed that Cassandra was simply abandoning her. She turned to her again, but already the woman had swung the gate shut and was relocking it. 'Cassandra...'

The housekeeper paid no attention to her plaintive call, slipping into her car and starting the engine, and Laura watched forlornly as she reversed back down the track.

Moments later she was alone.

Feeling desolate she pushed at the gate. It was made of vertical metal bars which offered her no chance of climbing over, and the fence was topped with razor wire. So she turned and gazed up the track. The wood looked unfriendly, yet there was nowhere else for her to go. Somewhere, amongst those brooding, unwelcoming trees, there was a house to provide her with some shelter, and hopefully some food.

Laura took a final glance back, then turned and began walking.

Chapter 16

The sun was warm on Laura's face as she made her way along the dusty track that led ever deeper into the wood. It was a beautiful morning, the sky a deep blue, the trees filled with singing birds. A squirrel ran across the track, pausing momentarily to stare at her before continuing on its way. Under any other circumstances she would have enjoyed every moment of it - but these were extraordinary circumstances.

And by far the worst thing about the whole unpleasant predicament was the sure knowledge that someone, or something, lay in wait for her in the sinister surroundings. Cassandra had hatched some diabolical plot and, although Laura didn't know exactly what the woman had in mind for her, there seemed little doubt that she was to be the victim.

Suddenly there was a commotion ahead. A bird fluttered up suddenly, squawking hysterically. Something had caused the creature to panic, but the question was, what? She listened intently, scanning the silent undergrowth and trees that lined the track on both sides, but could neither see nor hear anything to worry about. But still she was reluctant to advance. She looked back; there was nowhere for her to go in that direction except back to the gate, where she already knew there was no escape, and so she really had no choice but to press on.

She wondered if she might be safer heading into the trees, having noticed a few game paths that wound into their depths and that were wide enough to allow her passage. But she feared she might become hopelessly lost if she did, and if she was to find the house Cassandra had spoken about, she dare not stray.

She reached the spot where the bird had been spooked and peered amongst the trees. There was nothing unusual there; perhaps she was being too sensitive. After all, it was just a bird. There was nothing to be gained from creeping along, she told herself. It was time to move ahead.

As she turned with renewed determination to find the house Laura all but bumped into the man. She yelped from the shock and found herself looking into an unshaven face. He was big, over six feet tall with a broad chest and bulging biceps. He wore a T-shirt that was streaked with oil stains and a pair of dirty torn jeans, and his solid arms were decorated with tattoos.

'And where do you think you're going?' His voice was a low growl.

'I...' Such was the shock Laura's throat was dry, and she was unable to speak, so he grabbed her arm impatiently, his grip strong, his fingers digging into her wrist. 'D-don't, you're hurting me!' she managed to cry.

'Then answer my question,' he barked. 'What are you doing here?'

'Nothing,' she wailed, both at the brutality of his treatment, and at the injustice of it. 'I was just walking, that's all.'

'Didn't you see the signs?' he spat. 'This is private property.'

'I'm sorry,' she gabbled, her head in a spin. 'I wasn't doing any damage. I'm just walking.'

'No, you're trespassing,' he corrected belligerently. 'On private property.'

She tried to pull away from him but he was far too strong for her. She was aware of the way her tight dress was gaping at the top, and she saw his beady eyes drop to the creamy upper swellings of her breasts. 'Please,' she begged.

'Let me go. You're hurting me.'

And then he grinned a broad, gappy grin, and without warning stuffed a huge hand down into the bodice of her dress, possessively pawing a lusciously smooth breast before she could react defensively. Once Laura recovered a little from the shock and pace of the onslaught she tried to grapple the hand out of her clothing, but he was like a bear, immoveable, his muscles like iron.

He mauled her crudely, his calloused hand squeezing her poor breast, and while she was distracted and squirming the other fumbled for and groped her bottom through the short tight garment. 'Let go of me... *please*,' she implored, breathing heavily from her exertions and inadvertently pressing her breast more firmly into his greedy palm. And such was her confusion and panic she also did not notice that as she squirmed and squealed, demanding he let her go, something rigid and hard pressed against her hip.

'A gorgeous thing like you shouldn't wander around on your own,' he said, barely noticing her attempts to beat him off. 'Not on your own, and not on private property.'

'Wh-what do you want from me?' she spluttered.

'What I want is to teach you a lesson about what happens to trespassers around here. Now, let's get a proper look at you.' Then, without warning, he gripped her dress and savagely ripped it off, the material disintegrating and the buttons flying in all directions. Laura grabbed at it, trying her best to retain some vestige of modesty, but against the giant of a man she was helpless. He tugged again and the shredded garment simply fell away, leaving him holding a tattered rag as the naked girl tried desperately to cover her breasts and sex with her hands.

'Please, give me back my dress,' she implored, but he just sneered.

'What, this rag?' He tossed it aside, before adding menacingly, 'Now, you'll find out what we do to trespassers around here.'

She tried to dodge out of the way but he grabbed her arm once more, shoving her off the track and back against a tree. Laura could scarcely believe what was happening. She tried to fend him off, but he simply took her wrists in one hand and pinned them against the tree above her head, leaving her naked body open to his hungry gaze, her breasts heaving as she searched for breath.

With his free hand he began to maul her breasts again, taking his time a little more, sucking his teeth as he concentrated on the very pleasurable task of teaching her a lesson. He leered at her discomfort, running his hand down over her belly and lower, between her thighs. She tried to press them together, to deny him, but once again his strength was too much and a stubby finger wormed into her sex - which was shamefully already wet.

Laura gave a stifled gasp as he clumsily found her clitoris. Despite her fear and her aversion to him, his disgraceful treatment of her was exciting her more than she cared admit, and once again the image of Belita loomed large in her fertile imagination. As he slipped a finger into her she could scarcely suppress a moan, her sex muscles tightening involuntarily about the invading digit.

And her excitement was not lost on him as he crudely fingered her. 'You're loving this, aren't you?' he gloated.

'Wh-what do you want of me?' she gasped.

'I'm going to show you what we do to trespassers around here,' he said again. 'But first you're going to taste a real man's spunk.'

She stared at him, her eyes wide. 'Please let me go,' she pleaded. 'I wasn't doing any harm. I was brought here against my will and left...'

'Suck me nicely,' he cut over her rambling plea, 'and I might show a bit of sympathy.'

Laura looked up into the man's eyes, and it was clear she had no choice but to surrender. So she hung her head and murmured, 'Okay, I'll do whatever you say.'

'I know you will,' he sneered contemptuously. 'Now get down on your knees.'

He released Laura's wrists, allowing her arms to fall to her sides. She stood for a moment, staring down, and then slowly dropped to her knees.

Slowly, reluctantly, she reached up for his leather belt, her trembling fingers struggling with the heavy buckle. Once undone she fumbled the button of his jeans free, then slowly tugged down the zip.

The man said nothing more, but stood with his hands on his hips, breathing heavily as he stared down at the submissive beauty kneeling at his feet.

And so, summoning her resolve, Laura lifted her eyes and found herself gazing at a pair of tight briefs, stretched lewdly and monstrously. Knowing she had to go on, she curled her fingers into the waist of them and dragged them down, and as she did his cock sprang out in front of her spellbound face. It was large, the circumcised glans swollen and purple.

For a moment Laura's plight was forgotten as she stared at the jutting penis with clandestine admiration. She could smell him now, the scent of his arousal sending secret shivers of excitement through her. Hesitantly, she reached up, wrapping her fingers about the shaft, feeling it pulse with life as she squeezed it inquisitively.

'That's it, baby,' he murmured. 'Now suck it... go on, you know you want to.'

Laura paused, then inched her head forward, opened her mouth and took him inside. His cock tasted salty and slightly bitter, but the sensation of having it between her lips triggered a fresh spasm inside her vagina, making her juices flow still more. She began to suck him, feeling his cock stiffen further, swelling to fill her mouth completely.

He pressed his groin forward against her face until her nose nestled in his coarse pubic hair and he nudged the back of her throat, making her hum with suppressed alarm. 'Suck harder,' he ordered.

Laura began to move her head back and forth, her hair sweeping his tree-like thighs. Her hands closed about his hefty balls, squeezing them as he pumped his cock between her stretched lips. She found herself suddenly detached from the moment, her fears and anxieties momentarily forgotten as she sucked him avidly, her senses overcome with animal lust for the taste and feel of the stiff erection in her mouth.

He was fully aroused, his balls swinging against her chin, his cock forcing its way deeper and deeper into her throat. His fingers wormed into her hair, guiding the movement of her head to the tempo he required, Laura's breasts swaying firmly as she moved. She gripped his shaft, her fingers barely able to encircle its girth, moving the skin back and forth in time with his thrusts.

He came suddenly, a stream of seed erupting from the tip of his bursting penis as he grunted his total satisfaction. It filled her throat, momentarily threatening to overwhelm her, and then she swallowed enthusiastically, drinking his offering as fast as each diminishing pulse supplied it.

Breathing heavily he pulled his softening cock from her mouth, then pushed her backwards disdainfully. 'Not bad,' he said. 'Now, I think it's time you were punished for straying into this wood.'

'But I thought that if I sucked you...' Laura grumbled, though she knew it was pointless.

He sniggered gruffly. 'My, you are a naïve little thing, aren't you? Did you really think you'd get away without a thrashing?'

Laura looked up at him in alarm. He was staring down at her, an expression of scorn on his face, and that prompted her to do what she did next, even though there was no real avenue of escape.

She lunged at him.

Pushing him backwards the rucked jeans around his calves did the rest and, with a shout of rage he toppled over onto his back like a felled tree. Laura was on her feet in a second, but hadn't reckoned for the man's reactions. He grabbed her ankle. Laura gave a despairing lunge but he was far too strong for her and she collapsed in a heap. He scrambled to his feet, stood over her naked form, and slowly pulled up and fastened his jeans. Then he pulled the belt out of the loops and doubled it over in his fist.

'Right, little missy,' he hissed quietly. 'Time to teach you a lesson you won't forget.'

Chapter 17

Laura stood, one arm across her breasts, one hand protectively between her thighs, as she watched the man tear her dress into thin strips. There was absolutely no hope of escape now; he had buckled his belt around her neck and tied it to a branch. Her hands were free, but to remove it would be futile; he was much bigger and stronger than she was. So instead she tried to use her hands and arms to preserve what little modesty she had left, while anxiously watching him work.

'Hold out your hands,' he ordered. 'You heard me!' he barked when she hesitated. 'Hold your hands out in front of you, and do it now!'

The hostile tone of his thunderous voice made her flinch and obey hastily.

He grabbed a wrist, wrapping a strip of torn material around it and tying it tight, the makeshift bond biting into her tender flesh. Once both her wrists were soundly tied he undid the belt from the tree and dragged her to the side of the track. A tree had fallen there, it's branches caught in another so that its trunk was at an angle to the ground. Without ceremony the man pushed her forward over it, pressing her down against the rough bark. The stunted remains of a branch projected above her head and he dragged her arms up, tying them to it. Laura protested weakly.

'Shut up,' he cursed. 'And keep still.' He clutched her right ankle, binding a strip of cloth about it and securing it to a sapling on one side. Then he grasped the other, stretching her legs wide apart and knotting it to another young tree. Then, once she was secured, he stood back, chuckling as he surveyed his delicious captive.

Laura was tied face down over the tree, her hands pulled above her, her breasts crushed down against its coarse surface. With her legs spread wide as they were, her sex was forced down against the rough wood, her sensitive clitoris rubbing against a projecting nodule so that every slight movement caused an unwelcome shiver of delight to spasm through her.

The man removed the belt, then paused, allowing his fingers to trace the line of her spine, making her shudder slightly as he ran them down over her smooth flesh, sliding into the valley of her bottom. She gave a little gasp as they probed the heat of her sex, intruding deep within her. She struggled to stay still but, as he rotated his intrusive digit she felt her bottom move, pushing up against the hand as if inviting him to delve ever deeper, and he snorted derisively.

'Don't worry,' he mocked, 'you'll be getting plenty more than that soon enough. Right now I'm going to give you the punishment you deserve.'

He withdrew his finger, bringing a soft whimper from his helpless captive. She glanced over her shoulder. He was doubling the belt, running his fingers up and down its length, then reached out and pressed the swell of her buttocks, testing their softness. Then he drew back his arm.

Crack!

He brought the leather crashing down onto the tender young flesh of her bare behind with frightening force. As he struck she yelped as an extraordinary heat swept through her.

Crack!

He brought the belt down again, sweeping onto her poor bottom and bringing a new, more powerful spasm of agony that elicited another scream from her.

Crack!

Crack!

Crack!

He wielded the belt without mercy, laying stripe upon stripe across her pale flesh, each one stinging unbelievably.

Crack!

Crack!

Crack!

The tears were flowing freely down Laura's cheeks as she tugged frantically at her bonds, trying desperately to find a way to dodge the relentless rain of blows that swamped her.

Crack!

Crack!

Crack!

At last the punishment stopped. Laura's body was heaving with sobs, her bottom criss-crossed with angry red stripes that bore witness to every blow. The man loomed tall, staring down at his lovely captive as she slowly recovered her faculties. The pain in her rear was almost unbearable, her body glossed with perspiration. Yet, as the burning began to slowly fade, she knew just how aroused she was. Somehow the bondage and the beating had conspired to ignite once more the perverse passions Cassandra had discovered. As she lay across the crippled tree, naked and in broad daylight, her sensitive love bud pressed down against the rough bark, she was becoming more and more aware of her rising passions.

Smack!

Without warning the man brought the flat of his hand down across her bare behind, bringing back the pain of her punishment with a vengeance and making her cry out.

'Looks like a thrashing wasn't enough to teach you a lesson,' he said. 'Still, there's lots of time yet.'

'A-aren't you going to let me go now?' she asked timidly. 'I won't trespass here again, I promise.'

'Too right you won't. Not after we've finished with you.'

Laura's heart sank as she heard his words; how many others were there around like him? Clearly her ordeal was far from over.

Then she felt him undoing the bonds at her ankles. First one, then the other was released. She gave a sigh of relief and waited for him to free her hands as well, but he held her hips in a vice-like grip instead.

'Turn over onto your back,' he ordered.

'Couldn't you let my hands free?' she asked, wondering what he wanted of her next.

'Turn over!' he barked.

Slowly, awkwardly, the weary girl allowed him to twist her onto her back, her hands still fastened above her head. Once again she felt her cheeks glow as he eyed her breasts and the neat bush that covered her mons. Her flesh bore the red impressions of the bark. The surface had stimulated her nipples too, and as he nudged her legs apart she knew he could see how aroused and wet was her labia.

Once again her ankles were seized and tightly secured on either side of the trunk, and she glanced down at her firm, upwardly thrusting breasts, the nipples standing proud.

The man ran a hand over her breasts, smirking with intent as she sobbed timorously. He tested her bonds, and then nodded with approval.

'Right,' he said, 'I'll leave you here on display for a while.' He slid a finger into her succulent sex, making her writhe and moan softly. 'You won't get any satisfaction for a while, but I'm sure you'll enjoy anticipating what's coming to you.'

And with that he turned and sauntered off down the track, leaving a confused and frustrated Laura staring after him.

Chapter 18

Laura stared up at the swaying treetops above her, scarcely able to comprehend the seriousness of her predicament.

She contemplated the situation. Even when Cassandra outlined the ordeal she faced she hadn't been prepared for the reality of it. It was like the worst of Belita's ordeals; yet it was real, and there was more to come. The situation engulfed her like a nightmare, and there was nothing she could do to free herself from it.

So why was it making her so erotically excited? Why was her sex so hot and wet, her clitoris tingling with arousal? For the umpteenth time she wondered at the perversity and intensity of her feelings.

She lost all sense of time as she laid there, the sun warming her bare flesh, the gnarled tree trunk digging into her back and sending her uncomfortable reminders of the thrashing she had received. Every now and then she would think she could hear somebody coming, and she would tense in anticipation of being discovered as she was. Laura couldn't imagine what she would do should anyone come along, yet she knew that eventually she must be found, and the thought made her more apprehensive than ever.

There had been so many false alarms that, when she finally did hear the voices approaching she thought her mind was playing tricks with her again. Soon though she knew the voices were real enough, and went cold as she listened to them getting nearer and nearer. They were coarse male voices, occasionally guffawing at something amusing. Laura pulled frantically at her bonds trying desperately to free herself, but she remained securely tied.

Then she saw them; there were five, one of whom was the brute who found her originally and left her trussed to the tree. One of his companions had a beard and long greasy hair and, as he came closer, she thought she recognised him. Then she gasped. It was the gang of bikers! What on earth were they doing there? Surely it was all too much of a coincidence?

But all questions were banished to the back of her mind as the five loutish men gathered around her. Laura stared up at them, eyes wide. Like the one she sucked earlier, all were unshaven, tattooed and grubby. The one with the beard wore a denim jacket, the name *Jack* embroidered above one pocket.

'What are we going to do with her?' asked one of them. He was slimmer than the rest with long lank hair and a broken front tooth.

'Bloody hell, Tony, we can do what we like,' Jack said. 'Use your imagination.'

Tony sniggered. 'You want to fuck her right here?' he asked.

'Sure, Sam's already got her ready for it.'

'So who's going first then?'

'Wait,' Laura said anxiously, not liking the way they were talking about her. 'You can't do this.'

'Shut up,' Jack said dismissively.

'No, I...!' but her words were cut short as Sam clamped a hand over her mouth.

'You were told to shut up,' he hissed. 'You don't want that pretty little arse of yours thrashed again already, do you?'

Laura looked up at him, wide-eyed. No, she definitely didn't want to be beaten again. He obviously saw the fear in her eyes, and slowly let his hand slide down to her breasts. Laura gritted her teeth as she watched it mauling her, the fingernails black with grime, making her nipples harden as her lascivious nature responded again to his touch.

'See what I told you?' he said to his companions. 'The little whore loves it, just like the woman said she would.'

Laura froze at the words. So the brutes had been organised by Cassandra, and probably the earlier encounter in the diner, too. So now she was at their mercy the question was, what would they do with her?

As if in answer to her silent question Jack began to undo his jeans. 'I'm having her first,' he said, and the others nodded.

Laura watched him fearfully. There had been no question about asking her consent. They were using her, her opinions and requirements nothing to them. She was just a sex object - nothing more.

Already she could see the outlines of their penises pressing against the front of their jeans, and she shivered with anticipation of what was to come; despite her trepidation, her overriding emotion was one of intense and undeniable excitement.

Jack had eased his cock from his flies now, and Laura found herself unable to take her eyes from its throbbing length as he lazily worked his foreskin back and forth. He was rigidly erect, and she swallowed hard, knowing she was about to be fucked.

He straddling the tree trunk over which she had been so cruelly tied, his eyes fixed on her. He moved forward.

'Oh!' Laura couldn't suppress a whimper of lust as she felt the tip of his cock brush against her clitoris. She was aching with frustration, overwhelmed by a strong yearning for sex, and she lifted her hips, surrendering to the wanton passion that had been simmering for so long.

Jack gave a sudden thrust, and Laura cried aloud as his cock penetrated her. He thrust again, driving his rod deep into the heat and wetness of her vagina. Again she screamed at the delicious sensation his invading erection was bringing her. She knew what a slut she was making of herself as she moaned with pleasure, but her shame was overshadowed by her desire, and she squeezed her muscles around his cock as if trying to draw him deeper into her.

'She's loving it,' grinned Jack as he began thrusting against Laura's trussed body. 'She's loving every second.'

Every jab of his hips brought a fresh cry of pleasure from the helpless young beauty as she abandoned herself to her desires. Overshadowing the ignominy of her situation was the craving that such treatment always seemed to engender in her. She was overwhelmed by wanton desire as the rough stranger rutted on top of her, much to the delight of those watching. Sam had taken his penis out of his jeans again and was slowly masturbating, and Laura knew he would take her next.

Jack came, his face contorted with ecstasy, and that was enough for Laura who, with a cry, let herself go, her orgasm coursing through her body, her head rolling from side to side as she savoured a blissful release.

Then she felt Sam's erection impale her, and barely down from her first orgasm she felt a second beginning to build. The renewed vigour of the fresh violation was like an aphrodisiac to the lascivious beauty, and once again she abandoned herself to the sheer bliss of it all.

Sam showed no finesse at all, his cock pumping in and out of her like a piston while his collaborators encouraged him, their eyes filled with lust as they contemplated what was to come.

Sam erupted quickly, grunting his pleasure. Then he withdrew and a third erection invaded Laura's sex.

By the time all five had finished with her she was exhausted, completely sated, her body bathed in perspiration, her cheeks glowing.

'Can... can you let me go now, please?' she asked quietly, tentatively.

'That depends.' Jack looked round at his companions.

'Please let me go,' she pleaded. 'You've had what you wanted.'

Jack grinned. 'Oh, we're going to have a lot more of you yet,' he said.

Chapter 19

Laura rubbed her wrists, wincing at the tingling in her fingers as the blood was restored to them. With the throbbing of her bottom and the response of her body to the ravishing, she had scarcely noticed the discomfort of her bondage. Now though, the red marks around her wrists reminded her of how cruelly she had been bound.

A hand jerked her to her feet. She staggered slightly, unsteady on her legs after her ordeal, and instinctively she tried in vain to cover her nakedness with her hands.

'Zeke,' Jack said to one of the gang, 'you stay here and look after her while we go and get the bikes.'

'Sure,' he said. 'Go ahead. I can handle the little tramp.'

The four bikers set off along the track, leaving Laura alone with the balding member of the gang. Somehow, being alone with him seemed even more embarrassing, and she turned away, hugging herself.

'That was some thrashing Tony gave you,' he remarked, seeing the criss-cross of belt stripes laid across her bottom. 'Turn round, let me see you,' he ordered. At first she didn't obey, standing with her head bowed. 'Do as I tell you,' he snapped, 'or you'll be feeling my belt as well.'

Slowly, hesitantly, she turned to face him, her hands covering herself, her eyes cast down.

'Put your hands behind your head.'

She looked at him. 'Please...'

'Do it!'

Her cheeks glowing, Laura took her hands from her breasts and sex, raising and placing them behind her head, her trembling breasts thrusting, and her nipples standing out proudly.

'That's better,' he said approvingly. 'Now open your legs.'

With a sigh Laura moved her feet apart.

'Wider.'

Closing her eyes, Laura obeyed, her face crimson with shame.

'What's your name?'

'L-Laura,' she stammered.

'Laura,' he repeated, mulling the name over. 'Do you masturbate, Laura?' he asked suddenly.

'I beg your pardon?' she asked indignantly.

'You heard me. Do you masturbate?'

'Um... no - sometimes,' she blurted, confused and flustered.

'Masturbate for me now, Laura.'

'No, I...'

'Masturbate,' he insisted. 'Come on, or I'll have to use my belt on you.'

Knowing there was nothing else for it, Laura moved one hand down to her breasts, gently taking a nipple between finger and thumb, shivering slightly at the sensation. She glanced at Zeke, who was watching her intently.

Anxiously nibbling her lip, Laura flattened her hand against her soft flesh and began to slowly slide it down her body, over her flat stomach, hesitating for a second, then moving lower still. She felt the softness of her neat pubic hair, and then they were between her moist lips and touching the sensitised bud of her clitoris.

She gave a little gasp as a spasm of excitement shot through her body. Even after many draining orgasms she was still extraordinarily aroused, and the thought of Zeke's eyes watching her fingers as she explored the hot, damp cleft between her legs made her even more excited.

She looked into his eyes, and suddenly she realised how much she wanted to masturbate in front of him, to display her body lewdly to his gaze. She didn't understand the latent exhibitionism that was spurring her on to even more lascivious behaviour. All she knew was the churning in her belly, and the delicious sensation her fingers were giving her. She lowered her other hand from behind her head, cupping a breast and caressing the soft, pliant flesh.

'You're loving it, aren't you?' Zeke said, his voice thick with lust.

She was gradually moving her fingers with more urgency, her knees slightly bent, her hips slowly rotating. As she masturbated she formed an image in her mind of the lewd sight she was making, and felt her orgasm building inexorably... and then, to her immense disappointment she heard the sound of powerful engines. They were close by, the throaty roar telling her that the rest of the gang were approaching and was suddenly overcome by shame as she realised what she was doing. She tried to stop and cover herself again, but Zeke intervened.

'Keep going,' he barked. 'I want to see you come.'

Laura felt the tears well up in her eyes, wondering when the humiliation would end. Slowly, resentfully, she began to rub her bud once more, her body tense as she heard the motorcycles getting closer and closer.

All at once they appeared and were bearing down upon her. Laura was standing in the middle of the track, facing them, her legs apart, her fingers moving urgently in and out of her vagina as her passions began to overwhelm her once more. She could see the men were laughing as they neared, but she was too far gone to care. In fact, the new audience to her wanton exhibition served only to increase her desires and, once again, she felt her climax building as she frigged herself with vigour.

The four motorcycles came to a halt just in front of her and cut their engines.

'Bloody hell, Zeke,' Jack roared, 'she horny again already?'

Laura tried to blot their scorn from her mind. She couldn't stop now even if she wanted to; her desires were far too great.

She came with a low moan, her hips thrusting against her jabbing fingers as her body abandoned itself to her animal passions. All other thoughts were pushed from her mind by the sheer pleasure of her orgasm, her knees buckling as she continued to pump her fingers back and forth.

Then the sensation was ebbing, her reason began to return as the ardour drained from her, and she hung her head, unable to face her captors.

'Right,' said Jack. 'Time we were moving. Get her tied and we'll see if she puts as much effort into running as she does into wanking.'

Sam stepped forward, a coil of rope dangling from his hand. 'Hold your arms out,' he ordered.

Her heart thumping, Laura obeyed, and the man began wrapping the rope around her wrists. It was coarse and dirty and bit into her skin. He bound both together in front of her, leaving a long length free. Laura watched in some confusion as he tested the knots, took the other end of the rope and tied it to the back of one of the motorcycles, and his companions kicked their machines into deafening life.

And then it hit her what was happening. She began to protest, but even as she did the roar of Sam's engine drowned her words. Moments later he slipped the machine into gear and was moving forward, and Laura watched in horror as the rope tightened, and then almost jerked her off her feet.

Sam gunned his engine and accelerated, leaving the girl no choice but to run as fast as she was able after him. He seemed to be going at an impossible speed and it was all she could do to stay on her feet as she ran. The other bikers gathered around her, riding their machines so close that she felt sure they must hit her, before veering away, laughing at the sight of the naked beauty racing after Sam's machine, her breasts bouncing with every stride.

Whack!

Tony had pulled off his belt and he used it to flick her bottom, dragging a cry of pain and surprise from her as she struggled to stay on her feet.

Whack!

This time it was Jack who took advantage of the lovely target her buttocks afforded, his belt delivering a stinging blow.

On and on they went, the men never far from Laura, urging her on with jeers and whoops and painful blows from their belts. Laura was approaching the end of her tether, her lungs rasping, her legs aching terribly as she fought to stay on her feet. Then, just as she felt utterly exhausted and sure she would stumble and fall, they rounded a bend and a building came into view. Sam gave one last twist to the throttle, and then slowed to a stop.

Laura slumped, bent at the waist, bound arms dangling, her lungs bursting as she struggled to breathe. The bikes were silent, and she was vaguely aware of the gang dismounting around her. When her breathing gradually eased and she felt able to look up, her heart sank. Outside the large house was a row of gleaming motorcycles and there, lazing on the front steps, were at least a dozen more scruffy bikers.

Chapter 20

They were a motley crew, and Laura noticed they weren't all male. At least four of them were girls, wearing tight jeans or figure-hugging leathers.

Her gaze moved up to the building. It was an old country house that had seen much better days. Its imposing windows were broken or boarded up, and the tall chimneys were crumbling or strangled by ivy. The large front door was skewed on its hinges, and within it looked dingy and bare. All in all it was a strange and deserted spot, and she wondered how the bikers had found and occupied it.

Sam unfastened the rope from his bike, and then undid the knots that bound her wrists. As he did Laura heard the very faint sound of a car and a flash of reflected sunlight caught her eye. There was a road in the distance beyond a field, and she saw the roof of a car passing by.

The rope fell away and she was able to massage her numb wrists, aware that one of the bikers, a tall blond man with a ring through a nostril and a spider's web tattoo on his neck, was walking across towards her.

'Where did you find this, Jack?' he asked, his eyes devouring Laura's naked beauty.

'She's a trespasser, Leo,' Jack explained, and then Laura could have died as he went on to tell the gathered bikers the whole sordid tale, right from the moment she'd first been found by Sam.

Leo, still scrutinising her closely, sniggered and scratched his groin distractedly. He moved closer and grabbed her wrist, holding her at arms length and inspecting her. Laura knew she looked a sight, her hair tangled, her body streaked with sweat, her face glowing pink with exertion and embarrassment.

'Please, can you let me go now?' she asked quietly.

Leo sniggered again. 'From now on you speak only when spoken to, understand?' he said lethargically.

Laura opened her mouth to reply, then thought better of it.

'Little slut needs a wash,' declared one of the girl bikers. She had cropped red hair, wore jeans cut low on her hips and a short T-shirt, and her bare midriff revealed a pierced navel.

'You're right, babe,' Leo agreed, and Laura was immediately snatched by strong arms and dragged across to a pond that had once been part of an ornamental fountain. She was lifted bodily and, shrieking protestations, plunged into the cold water. Then a large hand clamped onto her head and held her beneath the surface for a few seconds before allowing her, gasping and spluttering, to lurch up and gratefully suck air into her screaming lungs.

Laughing heartily Leo dunked her again, and then allowed her to rise and scramble forlornly out of the pond, water dripping from her shivering frame, her hair plastered to her head and face, her flesh covered in goose pimples.

'That's better,' the girl biker who'd instigated the dunking gloated, cattily eyeing her up and down.

'Now,' said Leo. 'Time to find you something to wear.'

Laura looked up at him hopefully. At last somebody was showing some sympathy towards her. More than anything else she longed to be allowed some modesty. She watched with anticipation as another of the girl bikers approached holding a plastic carrier bag. She was petite with long blonde hair, and was wearing leathers that hugged her curves like a second skin. She held out the bag to Laura, who took it and glanced inside.

Instantly her gratitude turned to dismay as she surveyed the contents. It held nothing but some leather straps, like dog collars, with silver studs decorating them. Leo snatched the bag from her, reached in and pulled out the thickest of the straps, which had a ring attached to it. As he loomed over Laura her instinct was to shy away from him, but she stiffened her resolve and stood still while he strapped the collar around her throat, the ring at the front, and moved behind her to buckle it.

When satisfied he stepped away. 'Put your hands out in front of you,' he ordered.

Laura's heart sank even further, but she obeyed. He produced two more straps, shorter and thinner than the first, and proceeded to fasten them around her wrists, cinching them tight. One of them had a ring attached, the other a clip.

When the straps were secure he pulled her hands together and snapped the catch over the ring, fastening her wrists together. Then Leo nodded his satisfaction and undid them again.

There was one more item in the bag; a chain, with a leather loop at one end and a clip at the other. Leo fastened it to the ring at Laura's throat and tugged it, making her firm breasts quiver delightfully.

'Good,' he said, and then turned to the girl who had brought the straps. 'Take her inside.'

The girl pouted. 'What d'you want this trash for, Leo?' she sulked.

'Just shut up and do as I tell you,' he snapped. 'Put her in my room.'

The girl frowned, and then snatched Laura's lead. 'C'mon, slut,' she spat venomously, tugging it with unnecessary hostility.

Laura followed her amidst the lounging, lecherous, leering gang, through the large front door and into the house. The place was dingy and had a musty smell about it, and despite the bright warm sunshine outside, there was a damp chill in the air. There were no carpets, and the biker girl's boots echoed on the bare floorboards as she strode across the large room with her naked charge padding along behind.

As Laura followed the leather-clad girl along the hall and up a creaking flight of stairs, she pondered her fate. It all seemed pretty hopeless. Why was Cassandra so intent on putting her through such outrageous ordeals?

They walked along a wide landing and reached a door, and the biker girl ushered her charge into a bare room, with only a wooden table and a mattress for furniture. 'Stand by the table,' she ordered curtly, and Laura instantly did as she was told. 'Bend forward,' the girl pressed Laura's shoulder, forcing her down onto the hard surface, 'and lie flat.' Laura's breasts flattened against the tabletop.

The girl picked up some strands of rope from the floor and, looping them through the clip on Laura's wrist, pulled her arm across and secured it to the opposite table leg. She did the same with the other one, and then dropping to her knees, she fastened Laura's ankles to the table legs too. She was helpless, her shapely body trussed down against the unyielding wood, her limbs spread, her sex unprotected.

'There, that should keep you out of mischief.' The girl biker slapped Laura's bottom viciously with the flat of her hand, making her captive squeal and wince with pain, and then leaned down. 'They tell me you like a bit of rough treatment,' she whispered in Laura's ear. 'We'll have to see about that.'

And then she was gone, slamming the door behind her, leaving Laura alone in the room to ponder her fate. She strained to look about. To one side a large mirror was fixed to the peeling wall, and she stared at her image with trepidation, wondering how they intended to use her now.

The large house was silent. Time passed slowly. Thoughts drifted through her mind. They had not only taken away her clothes and her freedom, they had also taken her responsibility for her actions. She was at their mercy, unable to prevent them from doing what they wanted with her, and somehow that freed her to surrender to the perverse desires Cassandra had unearthed in recent weeks.

In an all too familiar way her nakedness, her helplessness, and the callous attitude of her captors were proving a powerful aphrodisiac. Even tied to the table, her situation desperate, she moaned softly as her desires began to overcome her. As her arousal increased her hips began an involuntary gyration and she pressed her pubis down against the solid surface of the table, trying in vain to stimulate her clitoris against it.

Just then the door opened with a crash that startled the trussed girl, her face turning bright scarlet as she craned round to see who was there. It was Leo, accompanied by Georgie. He was carrying a can of beer that he swigged from intermittently.

'Here she is, then,' he said, testing Laura's bonds, and then running a hand along her bare flank. 'And how's our little captive, hm?'

Laura jumped as she felt a finger penetrate her sex, making her gasp, her hips writhing at the unexpected intrusion. Leo laughed. 'I think she still needs a bit of loosening up,' he said.

The girl giggled. 'You gonna give it to her that way, Leo?'

'Sure, why not? C'mon baby, let's get started.'

They both moved round to stand by Laura's face, and as she watched the girl reached down and lewdly cupped his groin. 'You hard enough?' she asked casually.

'Sure - could do with a bit of lubrication, though,' he chuckled.

The girl smiled, then dropped to her knees. She tugged down his zip and reached inside. Laura found herself unable to tear her eyes from the throbbing cock that sprang from Leo's flies, the shaft bobbing up and down. Georgie took it in her fingers, moving the foreskin back and forth before opening her mouth and eagerly engulfing him.

As she began to move her head back and forth Laura watched, completely fascinated, and she swooned at the sheer eroticism of what she was witnessing.

'Jeez, that's good, baby,' Leo murmured.

Georgie raised her head, looking up at him. 'Why not forget the slut?' she said. 'You and me can get it on, Leo.'

'Nah,' he dismissed her offer, 'she's too good an opportunity to miss out on. According to the woman she's still a virgin, and you know how much I love to have me a virgin.'

The girl giggled again. 'Yeah, sure, I know.'

Laura was confused. She wasn't a virgin. Why would Cassandra say she was? And surely the pair knew what had happened in the woods? She watched anxiously as Georgie rose to her feet, still clutching Leo's rampant cock, and led him round behind her. Then she strained to look over her shoulder as the biker girl caressed her bottom and eased her buttocks apart. But all too soon her neck ached abominably and she had to rest her cheek back down on the table, closing her eyes in resignation.

'Okay Leo,' Georgie said, 'she's all yours,' and Laura's eyes flew open and she shrieked with shocked surprise as she felt the smooth head of Leo's cock probing insistently against her rear hole. Only then did she realise what was happening.

'No!' she cried, but already Leo was pressing against her, easing his bulbous helmet against the tight resistance of her anus. '*No...*' she cried again.

'Shhh... relax,' Georgie purred, her tone smug with satisfaction. 'You can't stop him, so relax and enjoy.'

The pressure increased. Laura's instincts told her to repel the invader, but she knew there was little point; so closing her eyes again she did relax, and allowed him the access he demanded.

She sighed a little sigh as she felt his rigid erection penetrate her bottom, gritting her teeth against the discomfort as he sank ever deeper until she was filled with stiff, pulsating cock. Tears filled her eyes, threatening to spill, but she forced herself not to cry out.

He began to fuck her bottom with long smooth thrusts, his penis pistoning back and forth between her buttocks, his strong hands clamped to her hips. For Laura it was the strangest experience yet of her journey into the depravities of Cassandra's world. During her sojourn in the room she had longed to feel a man relieving her frustrations, but to have him take her in such a manner was another matter altogether. Through blurred eyes she gazed across at the mirror, and there was no denying the eroticism of the sight that met her eyes. She moaned again; but this time it was a moan of pure bliss, such was the intensity of her response to what he was doing.

Leo was fucking her more and more frenetically, his hairy groin pounding down onto her quivering buttocks, the table rocking and creaking with every thrust. Laura clenched her fists in ecstasy, sensing the onset of his orgasm, and she tightened the muscles of her sphincter about his rod, urging him towards his climax.

He came suddenly, grunting with pleasure, his stiff penis pulsating as it pumped his seed deep into her rear. Once again it was like nothing she had ever experienced before, and she cried aloud as she came too.

Leo went on grinding against her until he was finally spent, leaning forward over her, still buried in her bottom. Then he withdrew slowly, bringing a gasp of relief from his naked captive as she felt him leave her. She stared at the mirror through teary eyes. He was grinning, an arm wrapped around Georgie's shoulder, who had clearly enjoyed what she'd witnessed.

'There you go,' she said with disdain. 'Now you really *have* lost your virginity!'

Chapter 21

It was late afternoon before Georgie finally appeared and released Laura from the table, but she was given little time to relieve the cramps of her imprisonment. No sooner had she regained her feet than Georgie snapped the lead to her collar, tugging it to ensure it was secure. Then she left the room once more, with her captive following obediently behind.

They only went a short distance along the landing to the next room, where grimy mattresses lay around the floor beneath rucksacks, battered cases, clothes and belongings; clearly the main sleeping area for the gang. Georgie took her across to a mattress in one corner, with a few items of clothing strewn across it.

Laura felt a surge of hope as she surveyed the clothing, and watched as the girl rummaged through her bags, willing her to pull out something that would cover her nakedness.

Georgie tossed her a pair of black knickers. 'Put those on,' she said.

Laura took them gratefully, stepping into and pulling them up.

'And these.' Georgie tossed her a pair of black leather boots. Laura caught them and, sitting down on the edge of the mattress, pulled them on. They reached her knees, and she zipped them up. The heels were very high, and she felt quite unsteady as she rose to her feet, just as Georgie tossed her something else. It was a waistcoat made of soft black leather, but even pulled tightly the two sides could not be made to meet in front. There was a single black lace dangling from each side, and Laura tied them into a bow between her breasts.

'Right, let's take a look.' Georgie grabbed Laura's lead and took her across to a dusty mirror that hung by the window. Laura eyed her reflection with dismay; surely she could have more to put on? The tiny panties hid almost nothing - the outline of her sex lips was clear - and the top was almost useless. The boots completed her discomfiture, somehow emphasising the fact that she was almost naked.

Georgie laughed. 'Not quite what you'd wear for a coming-out ball, is it?' she said. 'But it suits your character nicely. Can't wait to spread your legs for one of the guys, can you, slut?'

Laura didn't rise to the bait, but the colour in her cheeks betrayed the fact that Georgie had touched a nerve. It was true that, despite her shame, the explicit outfit was rekindling the desires she had felt earlier, and she knew that her sexy appearance would attract more than just the glances of the men. So it was with some trepidation that she followed Georgie down the stairs and outside.

The gang were all gathered about their motorcycles, and Laura sensed that something was about to happen. One of the machines roared into life and she watched in some trepidation, fearing she would be made to run behind once more, but Georgie led her across to where a gleaming machine stood by itself.

'You ever ride a bike before?' she asked bluntly, and when Laura shook her head she added, 'Just go with it on corners and hold on.'

The blonde released Laura's lead and straddled the motorcycle. To Laura it looked huge, and she wondered whether the girl would have the strength to handle it. She kicked the engine into life with ease, however, pulling the bike upright off its stand and gesturing to Laura to climb on behind her.

She obeyed hesitantly, placing a foot on one of the rests and then swinging her leg over. The leather seat felt cool and smooth between her bare thighs, the throb of the engine vibrating through her body. Georgie reached back and, taking hold of her lead, attached the end to a ring beside the saddle, ensuring that Laura couldn't dismount if she wanted to. Then Laura heard a roar and saw the rest of the bikes heading off down the track, and moments later they were following, the bike surging forward as Georgie dropped the clutch, and in no time at all they were through a gate and out on the open road.

Laura found herself exhilarated by the sheer thrill of speed as Georgie powered the machine expertly down the road, changing up quickly through the gears until they reached what seemed to the young captive an incredible rate. For the moment her troubles were forgotten in the elation of the ride. The bikers weaved about one another as they sped along, dropping the machines low into corners, the footrests scraping the road as they gunned their engines. They sped past other traffic, darting in and out of cars, taking what seemed to Laura incredible risks and laughing as they did so.

Soon they were speeding up a wide highway, Laura's hair streaming behind her in the wind as she clung tightly to the girl in front of her. Then they were slowing and swooping off the main road. Ahead Laura could see a building, and as they drew closer she saw a large sign across the top, *Cafe*. Outside were parked rows of motorcycles, some draped with leather-clad men and women.

Laura's heart sank as she felt the motorcycle slow. With all the excitement she hadn't really given a thought to where they were going, but as she surveyed the scruffy bikers' cafe she was reminded of the way she was dressed, and a cold fear clutched her stomach.

The bikes turned onto the small forecourt in formation and parked together, their engines cutting simultaneously. Then Georgie released Laura's lead from her collar, leaving it still attached to the bike, kicked down the stand and dismounted.

'Now listen, slut,' she said. 'You'd better behave yourself in there. All these guys,' she stabbed a thumb over her shoulder in the general direction of the cafe, 'are bikers like us. They're not going to be interested in anything but your tits and cunt, so don't go thinking you can get any sympathy from them.'

Laura glanced warily at the slouching rabble. 'Couldn't I just wait out here?' she asked, with little conviction.

'No, now get a move on or I might get annoyed,' Georgie said, her eyes glinting threateningly. 'And you wouldn't like me when I'm annoyed.'

Chapter 22

Laura's face was scarlet as she made her way towards the door of the diner, surrounded by her biker companions. As she reached the window she glimpsed her reflection, and groaned inwardly at what she saw. The black leather boots accentuated her slender legs, the tiny panties left nothing to the imagination, and the top strained valiantly to contain her breasts.

They reached the door and Leo pulled it open, then stood aside. 'Ladies first,' he said with an exaggerated bow.

Laura tried to hang back, but felt a dig in her ribs from Georgie. 'Go on, slut,' she hissed, 'get a move on.'

And so, taking a deep breath, Laura stepped inside.

The diner was noisy and crowded, the atmosphere heavy with tobacco smoke. The tables were strewn with mugs, empty plates, plastic ketchup dispensers and cheap cruets. Harsh fluorescent strips lit the place and dust and grease-engrained fans whirred precariously from the ceiling.

Eyes turned in Laura's direction, and for a moment the level of noise dropped. She felt her cheeks glowing as she made her way between the tables, urged on by Georgie, and soon they reached a spot at the counter where a number of stools were unoccupied. Georgie gestured to one of them. 'Sit there, and keep quiet.'

Laura had hoped they might find a table in a secluded corner where she would be less conspicuous, but the stool placed her on full view like a living exhibit. She eased onto the round seat, its plastic surface feeling cool against her buttocks.

'What's it to be?' asked a greasy individual from behind the counter, wearing an even greasier apron.

'We'll have the usual, Pete,' replied Georgie, sitting at the counter with Laura, along with Leo and three others of the motley gang. The rest were at other tables or chatting with their fellow bikers.

'Where'd you find this one, Georgie?' asked the man behind the counter, nodding at Laura as he started to dump some powdered coffee into a number of white mugs, most of which were stained and chipped.

'Oh, around,' she replied vaguely. 'Now get your beady eyes off her and get our order.'

'Sure,' he said, clearly not bothered by Georgie's belligerent attitude. 'Might be able to give you a bit of discount, though, if she's willing,' he added, throwing Laura an exaggerated wink and a wet kiss.

'I'll think about it,' Georgie said, lighting up a cigarette. 'Now, our order?'

The gang began to talk, and Laura simply sat quietly, trying to ignore the smirks of the staff and the occasional lewd comment thrown in her direction. Every now and then someone would push past her, taking the opportunity to squeeze the soft flesh of her bottom, the physical contact making her shiver slightly.

A mug of stewed coffee was slapped down in front of her, some of it slopping over onto the counter, along with a plate of fried food swimming in fat. Despite its unappetising appearance it made her realise just how hungry she was, and she shovelled the meal down, forgetting her troubles briefly as she washed it down with the bitter, dark coffee.

She finished the meal and Pete took away the plate. She had hoped the gang wouldn't linger once they had eaten, but they showed no signs of being in any hurry to leave, smoking and chatting amongst themselves, seemingly oblivious to their captive.

After a while Laura became aware of being watched by someone in particular who was taking more interest in her than most.

She turned, and there he was - a handsome man with a day-old growth of stubble and fair hair, neatly cut. But it was his eyes that captured Laura's attention; deep-set and intense, they seemed to stare into her very soul. She turned away, but was still acutely aware of his gaze upon her, and she felt the blood rise in her cheeks once more.

Then a hand touched her shoulder, making her jump. She swung round to see him standing next to her, so close she could smell his maleness, the scent making her shudder with desire.

'Who are you?' he asked, his voice like velvet, but like his eyes there was a dangerous edge to it.

'I... my name's Laura,' she stammered.

He eyed her up and down, his gaze straying to her breasts. 'Get up,' he said.

There was a proprietary air about him that made the submissive girl obey without question. She climbed down from the stool and stood in front of him, trying her best to adjust her top so that it gave her some concession to modesty under his piercing gaze.

'Bend over, across the stool,' he ordered.

Laura looked questioningly at Georgie. The blonde had paused momentarily in her conversation to see who it was with Laura, but she turned back and continued her conversation with Leo, apparently unconcerned.

'Come on, get a move on,' the man said.

Laura threw a final glance at Georgie, then turned and draped herself forward over the plastic top of the stool, raising the round cheeks of her bottom invitingly.

For a moment he said nothing, then she gave a start as she felt powerful hands grasp her buttocks, pulling them apart. Laura's instincts told her to protest, but the fact that Georgie had made no attempt to prevent him from touching her told her that to do so would be in vain. Instead, she remained where she was, her eyes tightly closed, her mind in turmoil as she thought of the many eyes that were witnessing her torment.

'Lift your backside up,' he ordered.

Once again Laura obeyed with some reluctance, slowly lifting her buttocks upward.

'Oh!' she gasped as she felt a finger worm its way inside her panties and run along the slit of her sex. '*Ah...*' She gave an involuntary little moan as he found her clitoris, his finger pressing the bud, exploring her intimately. And then the finger withdrew.

'Okay, stand up,' he said.

Laura eased herself from the stool and turned to face him, her face burning with shame.

'You're not promised, then?' he asked.

'Promised?'

'You don't bear anyone's mark,' he explained, still somewhat cryptically.

'I-I'm sorry, I don't understand.' Laura felt foolish for not knowing what he was talking about.

The man turned to Georgie. 'She's a chattel, yeah?'

Georgie smiled and shook her head. 'No, Spanner. I can see why you'd think so, though. She'd make a bloody good one.'

'So what's she doing here dressed like that?'

'We're just taking control of her as a favour for somebody,' Leo explained. 'She's having a little holiday with us, aren't you, slut?'

Laura said nothing, her eyes downcast. She didn't understand what they were talking about.

Georgie giggled. 'You'd like to see her with your own mark on, wouldn't you Spanner?' she said.

'If she had the right temperament, I might,' he admitted.

'What do you think of the idea?' asked Leo, turning to Laura.

'I'm sorry, I don't understand what you're talking about,' she said apologetically.

'A chattel is a personal slave,' Leo explained. 'A chick who gives herself to a biker and lets him do what he wants with her.'

'D-do what he wants?' she gasped, her eyes wide.

'Sure,' Georgie said. 'In the old days girls weren't allowed in biker gangs. Someone like me could only become a part of this scene by taking a biker's mark and becoming his chattel.'

'You mean, like being his girlfriend?'

Spanner laughed. 'Not exactly,' he said.

'You see,' went on Georgie. 'The mark simply signified ownership. It meant the girl had to obey the guy whose mark she wore. The biker could give her to anyone he liked. The chattels were sent away for weeks at a time, often to foreign gangs in Europe. There they'd be treated as slaves and made to work in brothels. Sometimes they wouldn't see their owner for months, or even years.'

'But they'd carry his mark,' said Spanner.

'That's what Spanner was looking for,' explained Leo. 'If you were a chattel you'd have your owner's mark tattooed on your arse, or wear a ring and tag in your cunt. You should be flattered that Spanner was so interested.'

Laura eyed the handsome biker, wondering what it might be like to bear his mark, and was surprised to discover that, far from disgusting her, the idea was oddly arousing.

She shook her head. It was silly. Soon the whole ordeal would be over and she would be back in the safety of her guardian's house. Then she would be able to put the whole nightmare behind her and forget that chauvinist louts like Spanner existed. Meanwhile, she must try her best to endure the indignities being heaped upon her.

'Hey, Georgie, how about settling the bill?' called the man behind the counter, waving a piece of paper at the biker girl.

She took it from him and studied the scrawled figures, then glanced at Laura. 'What about that discount you promised?' she said.

'Let me take her round the back and I'll halve the bill,' he leered.

'What d'you think, Spanner?' asked Georgie. 'Is that a fair deal?'

'If she was my chattel, I'd go for it,' he said.

Georgie pondered his opinion for a moment, and then made her mind up. 'Okay, come on, slut, you're going to earn your keep.'

Laura stared at the girl, then at the grinning man behind the counter, noticing with horror the slight tenting of his apron, and this time she didn't need an explanation to know what was going on. She glanced desperately about for some support, but saw only unsympathetic faces.

Then Spanner grabbed her waist, lifted her up onto the bar and swung her round to face Pete. She tried to hang back, but Spanner gave her a shove and she fell forward into the arms of the waiting man, and the cheers of the other bikers were ringing in her ears as she was led out through a door at the back.

She found herself in a small storeroom, and for the first time she studied him properly, and shuddered. He was beyond middle age, grubby, and definitely not remotely attractive in any way. How on earth did she keep getting herself into such awful predicaments?

He reached out and ran his stubby fingers down her cheek; they smelt unpleasantly of cooking fat. 'What's a pretty little thing like you going round dressed like that for?' he leered. 'In this place that's just begging for it.'

Laura made no reply, her gaze dropping to the floor, and he moved back and sat on a bench.

'Strip,' he said suddenly, and Laura looked at him with a pleading expression. 'You heard me. I want a proper look at you before I screw you.'

Had Laura really reached a point where she obeyed any man who spoke to her? Was she now such a slut that she stripped on demand, no matter who was telling her to? Her shoulders slumped; she knew that was precisely what she had become. They had sucked any fight from her and reduced her to a slave of their desires.

And yet, she pondered, it was a sweet submission. Even now, in the back of the squalid diner with a stranger, her body was stimulated beyond belief, ready to take his cock in any way he demanded. In all her life she had never felt so alive than when Cassandra introduced her to her own desires and, as her fingers moved to the lace that held the straining waistcoat together across her breasts, she knew their trembling was due to excitement rather than fear.

The skimpy garment burst open to reveal her mouth-watering breasts to the man's hungry gaze, and he slapped his lips together as though tasting the succulent flesh. The constant chafing of her nipples against the leather had caused them to harden, and they stood proud and erect, quivering slightly as she awaited the next order.

Following his unspoken demand she shrugged the waistcoat off, and it fell to the floor behind her. Then her hands dropped to her hips, and she slipped the tiny panties down her legs and off, kicking them aside.

The man laid back along the bench, his eyes drinking in her nudity. He beckoned to her and she obediently moved to his side, blushing at the way his bulging eyes were blatantly devouring her, aware that her sex lips were shiny with moisture.

'Suck me,' he ordered. The words should have shocked Laura, but they didn't, and she meekly sank to her knees beside the man, peeled aside his apron, opened his trousers, and fumbled inside to tug out his cock. His own arousal was easy to see, his thick, circumcised stalk spearing up from his lap, the helmet smooth, purple and shiny. Without pausing Laura lowered her head and took it between her lips, her senses drowned in his masculine scent and taste as she began to fellate him. She sucked hard at his stiff organ, her hair curtaining her face and sweeping his lap as she moved her head up and down, her lips sealed tightly around the turgid shaft. He groaned as she performed on him, pressing his groin up to meet her face.

'Shit, that's good...' he croaked. 'On top now,' he said suddenly. 'Quick - I want to fuck you.'

Once again Laura's response was unquestioning. She rose, elegantly swung a leg over his waist and hovered, facing him, a foot on either side of the bench. And then supporting herself with one hand on his rotund belly, and gripping his cock with the other, she slowly sank down, impaling herself, her eyes closing and her glistening wet lips parting slightly as she sighed in unison with the inexorable penetration by the rigid spear of flesh.

Secretly savouring the invasion she used her fingers to spread her labia, easing him into her, soft whimpers escaping her lips as she settled lower and lower until she was settled on his lap.

Then, after a brief pause and a deep breath, her breasts swelling as she filled her lungs, she began to move.

The sensation was exquisite, her sensitive clit rasping against his shaft with every rise and fall of her hips. Laura instantly forgot all her inhibitions as the sheer pleasure of being fucked overwhelmed her, and she moved with ever-increasing fervour, her head thrown back so that her hair spilled down and swept her back.

Suddenly the door burst opened and Laura found herself staring at a grinning face. It was a young cook, no more than a teenager. He stopped short, his eyes fixed on Laura, but she was beyond shame now, and even though she knew she was putting on a lewd display for the young man it seemed to spur her on, and she thrust her breasts forward and threw her head back, revelling in her exhibitionism.

He came with a groan, and then she was coming too, moaning as she worked her body up and down in a frenzy of desire, her whole being focussed on the erupting cock embedded in her vagina. He seemed to come and come, each spurt from his erection bringing renewed pleasure until she could stand it no longer and, with a cry, collapsed forward over him.

They lay there for a few minutes, their passions slowly subsiding, then for no apparent reason he pushed her onto the floor.

'Get the trollop out of here,' he ordered the youth.

The lad's grin broadened. 'Come on, you,' he said, took her arm, yanked her to her feet and dragged her towards the door.

Laura pulled back, her passion suddenly turned to shame as she contemplated what he had witnessed. 'My clothes!' she protested.

The lad paused, then reached down and scooped up the waistcoat and panties. 'Call these clothes?' he said scornfully, and then pulled her through the door, his strength overcoming her attempts to pull back. As they emerged into the diner she grabbed for her garments, horrified at the thought of being seen naked in such a place. But he simply held them up out of her reach, his laughter being joined by that of the customers as they realised what was happening and turned to watch her strain to reach the hand held high above his head.

'Please give them to me,' she begged, her face glowing scarlet as more and more eyes were turned in her direction.

'All right,' he said. 'Here you are,' and tossed them over the counter, and Laura watched in dismay as the waistcoat and panties flew in an arc across the diner and landed on the floor between the tables. He released her arm and she stared wildly about; there was nowhere to hide - nowhere to go.

A cheer went up as she scurried around the counter and dashed across to where her clothes were lying. Her face was the colour of a beetroot as she snatched them up, struggling into the brief panties then pulling the waistcoat on, covering her breasts as best she could. Then, with jeers and applause ringing in her ears, she made her way, shamefaced, back to Leo and Georgie who still sat on their stools at the counter.

Chapter 23

The motorcycle sped along the road, its engine roaring as it left the diner, fading into the distance. On the pillion seat Laura clung to the back of Georgie, relieved to be getting away from the place.

They hadn't lingered long after her emergence from the back room. There had been one more brief incident, however. As she was waiting for Georgie to settle the balance of the bill, Spanner had approached her again. He stood in front of her, his muscular frame dwarfing her petite one, running a hand through her hair.

'Enjoy that, did you?' he asked.

Laura avoided his eyes. 'You were the one who decided my fate,' she accused quietly.

'You didn't put up much of a fight, though, did you? Was he a good fuck?' Laura didn't answer, but Spanner was insistent. He cupped her chin and raised her face to his. 'Did you come?'

She reddened. 'I...'

'Well, did you?'

'Yes,' she whispered.

'You're an odd one,' he mused, shaking his head.

Georgie had joined them then, and Laura looked hopefully towards the door.

'You want her, Spanner?' the biker girl asked, making Laura's heart sink.

'Sometime,' he said. 'Maybe.'

'When she's got your mark on her pretty arse?'

'If she had my mark, I'd make sure everyone saw it. She doesn't need those knickers.' Then, unexpectedly, he bent forward and kissed her, his tongue forcing its way into her mouth. For a moment she resisted, pushing against his chest and attempting to keep her lips closed, but she couldn't. She held her body stiff, trying to suppress emotions his intimacy was engendering inside her, but his powerful masculinity was too much. As his tongue snaked into her mouth she was suddenly overwhelmed by desire, melting into his arms and surrendering herself to him.

He kissed her long and hard, clamping his brawny arms about her slender body and pulling her close as his lips crushed down against hers. He slid a hand up her belly and, pulling the cord on her waistcoat, closed his fingers over her breast, kneading the soft flesh and delighting her even more. His boldness melted her last remnants of resistance, so she didn't care that her breasts were revealed to everyone watching, so involved was she in the passion of the embrace.

As abruptly as it had started the kiss came to an end and Laura staggered back, still slightly stunned by the biker's passion. For a moment she just stood there, staring wide-eyed up into his face. Then she heard the whistles of the other bikers and remembered that her breasts were bare. Flustered, she pulled the waistcoat together again and fumbled with the cord.

Georgie laughed. 'You really do fancy taking a chattel for yourself, don't you Spanner?'

The big biker smirked back. 'There's nothing like upholding old traditions,' he said. Then, with a final glance at Laura, he turned and walked away.

Since then Laura had been unable to erase him from her mind, and she wasn't sure why. After all, he was just another uncouth yob who wanted to abuse her, to make her his plaything to be used at will, giving her to other men on a whim, even allowing her to whore for him. Any man who thought of a woman like that wasn't worth considering, was he? So why did the idea make her feel so aroused? And why did she feel flattered that he had singled her out to take on the role? Not for the first time since beginning her sexual awakening, Laura found her thoughts extremely muddled.

She was woken from her reverie by a drop in the engine note of Georgie's motorcycle and the sensation of the machine slowing. She glanced over the biker's shoulder and realised they were approaching the big house.

That night Laura had little sleep, finding herself being passed from mattress to mattress as the bikers took advantage of her naked and helpless body. She lost count of the number of orgasms that coursed through her as man after man made use of her before passing her on. It wasn't until the early hours that they had at last finished with her and she was allowed to sleep, curled up on a bare mattress, her collar chained to a heavy metal radiator, her wrists bound behind her.

She awoke to find herself alone. Her limbs were stiff, her hair a tangled mess, and as she sat up her heart sank with the knowledge that her ordeal was far from over. She gazed up at the ornate but decaying plasterwork on the ceiling, pondering her fate.

The previous day and night had been the most extraordinary she had ever experienced; her modesty discarded she was chastised, abused, and violated by men and women who treated her as no more than a slave and a whore. She should be a hysterical wreck, yet she was calmly analysing her situation, and though she found it difficult to admit to herself, though tired and aching, she felt more alive than she had ever done before. Were it not for the fact that her hands were trapped behind her, she may well have touched herself in the scant privacy the bikers had allowed her.

Georgie appeared about an hour later, kicking open the door and wandering across to where she sat, gazing down at the young beauty.

'So, you're awake are you?' she said. 'That was quite a performance you put on last night. I've never seen anyone with such an appetite for a stiff cock. How many orgasms did you have?'

Laura didn't answer, her eyes avoiding those of her captor, so Georgie crouched down and released the lead from the radiator.

'On your feet, slave,' she ordered. 'It's time you cleaned yourself up.'

94

Laura feared they might make her bathe in the cold pond again, but to her surprise the biker girl led her to a large bathroom with an old shower and toilet.

'There's soap and shampoo,' she said brusquely. 'Try to make yourself look presentable. I'll be back in half an hour.'

Laura was even more surprised to find hot water running from the taps, and the luxury of it cascading down and soothing her weary body, combined with the scented soap and shampoo, was wonderful.

She washed thoroughly, dried herself, brushed her hair out before a mirror, and by the time Georgie returned she was feeling very much better.

'Good, at least you don't look like a guttersnipe whore any more,' observed the biker, eyeing her naked form from head to toe. 'Come on.'

Laura hung back uncertainly. 'Couldn't I have some clothes?' she asked.

Georgie sniggered. 'Forget it,' she said. 'The guys like seeing you bare-arsed. Now hurry up and follow me.'

Laura went with her down to a room where it seemed some sort of breakfast had recently been served. There were a few slices of bread on a table, alongside them was a large frying pan containing a couple of overcooked sausages, congealing in their own fat as they cooled, and beside that was a pot of coffee. Slouched around the room were a few bikers, some still eating or drinking, and they looked up and grinned as she entered. Recognising most of them as having fucked her the night before, Laura avoided their eyes as best she could.

'Go on, help yourself,' said Georgie. 'Then you can get to work cleaning this place up.'

Laura was starving, so despite the continuing embarrassment of being naked, she placed a couple of the tepid sausages between two slices of bread and devoured the lot eagerly, washing it all down with a cup of lukewarm coffee.

Afterwards she was put to work clearing the table and sweeping the room, and was then given other menial tasks by Georgie. And she didn't really mind, because the work helped keep her mind off her predicament, though the bikers frequently reminded her of it. Every now and again one would encounter her in one of the corridors and take advantage of the situation by groping her, but most of them seemed to be absent, their bikes missing from the drive.

In the afternoon she was put in the charge of four of the male bikers who attached a lead to her collar and took her off into the wood. There, despite the injustice, she was tied to a tree, the rough bark digging into her flesh while they thrashed her bare behind with a belt.

Once her buttocks were glowing they cut her down and took it in turns to fuck her. They made her straddle them as they lay in the grass, working her up and down, her breasts trembling as she followed their grunted demands and rode them to completion.

In the evening she was taken back to the diner, clad in brief underwear and black hold-up stockings, much to the delight of the other bikers. Once again they sat her at the counter where everyone could see her.

As she ate she found herself searching the room for Spanner. At first she thought he wasn't there, and found herself unaccountably disappointed by his absence. Then her stomach tightened as she caught sight of him sitting at a table in a gloomy corner of the room.

He had an arm around Georgie's shoulder, and the two of them were laughing, looking very comfortable together. Laura felt an unexpected pang of jealousy as she witnessed the apparent intimacy of the pair, though she couldn't rationalise the emotion. After all, Spanner was just the worst kind of lout - wasn't he? And his attraction towards her, not as his lover but as his slave, was hardly flattering.

This time Laura did not have to do anything more than eat her meal and remain obediently quiet on the stool, and so it was with immense relief that she found herself being led back to Georgie's machine, even though she was, somewhat bizarrely, still put out by the fact that Spanner had paid her no attention whatsoever.

Chapter 24

The days passed, and Laura settled into her life as a slave to the bikers. Every day she would be set menial tasks to perform, and soon became familiar with the obedience required of her. Apart from the occasional trip to the diner in the evenings, the gang kept her naked at all times. This nudity was by far the most trying part of her ordeal; her natural modesty meant that she was perpetually embarrassed at having to display herself to all and sundry.

The bikers used her when they wanted, sometimes coming upon her in the middle of a chore, invariably wringing an orgasm from the licentious young beauty. They used her vagina, her mouth, and occasionally her anus would be the target of their desires.

The visits to the diner, too, were a torment for her, knowing that she would be dressed in the most titillating way Georgie could devise, so that she was the centre of attention amongst the bawdy rabble who frequented the place.

And then there was Spanner. There was something about the powerful man that held a fascination for Laura, even though she told herself that she loathed his chauvinism and the contempt with which he treated her. Each time she was led into the noisy, steamy, smoky establishment, she would find herself searching the leering faces for his. Sometimes he would speak to Georgie or other members of the gang, and occasionally there would be words for Laura too. But more often than not he would ignore her, and that would make her angry and frustrated, although she couldn't understand why.

She lost track of the days, so that she could not really judge how long the nightmare had been going on, or anticipate how much longer it would continue. Day followed night and night followed day, and indignity followed indignity, so that it became almost commonplace to find herself tied naked to a tree or to some piece of old furniture while her captors enjoyed themselves with her body.

Then, one afternoon, something happened to change her strange routine.

It was a warm day. About half the bikers were off somewhere and she had just returned from a naked walk in the woods, during which she had been obliged to suck her three escorts until they came in her mouth. Upon their return the men pulled chairs out onto the grass where Laura served them cans of beer, then knelt beside Jack's chair, scarcely listening while he, Sam and Tony discussed their motorcycles.

It was she who first spotted the strangers approaching, initially just shapes moving behind the more distant of the trees down the drive. She squinted into the distance, confused by the sight. She knew there were only three other bikers around, and she could see them tinkering with their machines about fifty yards away, in between her and the approaching figures.

Slowly the newcomers neared; there were three of them, two men dressed in casual clothes and a woman. From the distance it was difficult for Laura to make them out properly, but she could see that the woman was dressed in dark slacks and a bright yellow blouse. She had long blonde hair and a slim figure, and she was strolling along confidently between the men.

Laura felt uneasy and instinctively she tried to rise, but Jack had hooked the end of her lead around the leg of his chair, trapping her where she was.

'What the...?' he said as he felt her tug on the chain.

'Someone's coming,' she warned, her voice barely a whisper.

Jack squinted in the direction she was looking. Already the other bikers had seen the new arrivals and had risen to their feet, watching them as they approached.

'I'd better go inside,' Laura said hastily, uncertain of what was happening. 'Before they see me.' She tried to rise again, but was pulled down by another sharp tug on her lead.

'Just stay where you are,' growled Jack.

'But...'

'And shut the fuck up,' he added. 'Or I'll thrash that bare arse of yours.'

Laura settled back to her knees, watching with growing trepidation as the three strangers drew closer. The three other bikers were walking towards them now, Zeke in front. They stopped, still some way off, talking together. Laura prayed they were telling the trio that they were trespassing and were ordering them out of the wood, but her heart sank as she saw the three bikers turn and accompany them towards the house - and to where she was kneeling, submissively tied to a chair.

Laura simply wanted to run and hide, such was her chagrin at being found in such a subservient fashion, and she knew the moment she had been spotted; the woman suddenly pulled up short, staring directly in her direction, and moments later her two companions had also fixed their eyes on the naked, blushing girl. A brief conversation ensued, and she knew the woman was questioning what was happening. Then, to her complete mortification, the group began walking towards them again.

As they drew close Laura shot a quick glance at the woman's face. She was indeed attractive, her flowing blonde hair framing a beautiful, if rather arrogant face, the pretty lips pursed as she eyed her. And her companions' faces showed undisguised interest, mixed with amusement, at the sight she made. They were slightly older than the woman and expensively dressed, their whole demeanour reflecting the confidence of their female cohort.

Laura knelt in silence, her eyes cast down as Zeke introduced the new arrivals to his fellow bikers. It seemed their car had broken down about a mile away and, seeing the house through the trees, they had decided to search for some help.

'We'll take a look at the car in a minute,' said Jack. 'Meanwhile, have a rest and a drink.' He nudged Laura with the scuffed toe of a heavy boot. 'Go and get our guests some chairs and beers,' he ordered.

He released her lead and she rose to her feet, her face bright red as she found herself the centre of attention once again. She turned, aware of the eyes on her bare bottom as she made her way to the house.

Having produced three folding chairs she went back for the drinks, and felt more exposed and more ashamed than ever, handing the cold cans to the visitors as they sat fully and expensively clothed. It was a relief to be able to retreat to Jack's side, though she would have much preferred to go back into the relative safety of the house.

The conversation continued. The woman, it transpired, was an interior designer; her two companions her boyfriend, Joel, and her business partner, Andrew. They were on their way to a conference, but were in no particular hurry. Laura wished desperately that they would leave, but they showed no signs of wanting to do so.

Eventually, however, and to Laura's immense relief the woman, whose name was Jacqueline, rose to her feet.

'Well, we'd better press on if we're going to get the car fixed,' she said.

'Zeke and Sam'll go with you and take a look at it,' Jack said. 'If anyone can sort it out, they can. And if they do get stumped, there's a garage a few more miles down the road.'

'Sure,' said Zeke, with a noticeable glint in his eye. 'We'll do that for you.'

'And you can ride with me,' Sam offered eagerly, his eyes roaming over the classy lady.

'Well, I...' the woman started uncertainly, and then added, smiling, 'Okay, I haven't been on a motorcycle since I was a teenager. It'll be fun.'

'And what about us?' asked Joel, eyeing the two bikers suspiciously as he indicated himself and Andrew. 'I think we'd better come too.'

'Nah,' Jack dismissed his suggestion with a wave of a hand and a casual swig from his can. 'You can wait here and enjoy your beers.'

'I'll need a helmet,' the woman said with increasing enthusiasm. 'Have you got a spare?'

'Yeah,' Zeke said, and then turned to Laura. 'Take the lady inside and find her one,' he grunted.

Laura looked at him with some dismay; so far, apart from the humiliation of having to serve the drinks, she had remained on the periphery of the small impromptu gathering, but now, as Zeke pulled her to her feet, she realised that she would, for a short time at least, be alone with the confident and rather arrogant female.

And her trepidation increased when Zeke handed the lead to the woman, who cast a contemptuous eye over her.

'She's house trained, I take it?' she said.

Zeke snorted. 'If she causes you any bother, let us know. Show her your backside girl.'

Laura, her face crimson, turned to let the woman see the red stripes that criss-crossed her bottom.

'Hmm,' said the woman, examining the marks of Laura's punishment. 'Looks like you run a tough regime here.'

'Only with sluts like her,' replied Zeke. 'Gotta make sure she behaves.'

'Come on then,' said Jacqueline, tugging at Laura's lead. 'Show me where these helmets are so we can rescue my poor beloved car.'

Once inside the house Laura led the way up the large staircase, only too aware of the perfect view her pert behind offered Jacqueline. Somehow, of all the trials she had been forced to endure, submitting to such a haughty woman was possibly the most difficult, sensing nothing but contempt from her as she showed her into the bikers' sleeping room.

'There are plenty of helmets here,' she said meekly.

Jacqueline looked around. 'Get me that one,' she ordered, indicating a particular helmet on one of the mattresses. 'Put it on me.'

Laura moved close to the woman and placed the helmet on her head. As she fiddled with the chinstrap she was aware of her stiff nipples brushing lightly against the woman's top.

'Don't stand so close to me, you little slut,' Jacqueline whispered spitefully. 'Don't you have any shame?'

Laura didn't answer, her cheeks glowing as she finished the task and stepped back.

Jacqueline checked the helmet in the mirror. 'This will do, I suppose,' she said, as though getting bored, and then she looked around the room again. 'Do they fuck you in here, on these mattresses?' she asked bluntly.

Taken aback by the frankness of the question, Laura did not know what else to do but nod dumbly in reply.

'And the others watch?'

'S-sometimes,' she stammered, loathing the condescending woman for goading her so.

'And don't you feel ashamed, giving yourself like a common slut?'

'I... I have to do as I'm told.'

'Why, are you some kind of prisoner here?' the woman said sarcastically.

'Well, I am a kind of slave,' Laura muttered honestly.

'A slave?' the woman snorted. 'What rubbish. They can't keep you here against your will, can they?'

'I suppose they can, because I'm not allowed to leave,' Laura answered simply.

'Of course you are,' Jacqueline derided. 'Look, there are clothes in here; put something on.'

Laura shook her head. 'No, I can't.'

'Yes, you can,' she insisted, and picked up a discarded dress. 'Here, put this on.' Then she completely knocked Laura sideways by adding, 'And I'll take you home, if you'd like that.'

Laura stared at the dress, then at the woman; she wanted nothing more than to put it on and to hide her nudity. But she dare not. If she surrendered to the woman her identity would be at risk and, more importantly, the identity of her guardian, and that she could not allow. Better to remain naked and enslaved until Cassandra decided the game was over, than to admit to Sir John what she had been doing and to risk embroiling his name in a sleazy scandal.

'No,' she said resolutely, despite her real yearning to put some clothes on and get away from the place. 'I want to stay here.'

'You *really* want to stay here?' Jacqueline asked, clearly disbelieving her.

Laura hesitated for a few seconds, knowing an opportunity to escape was rapidly slipping away, and then nodded slowly. 'Yes,' she said. 'That's what I really want.'

The woman shook her head. 'Then you are nothing more than a common slut, aren't you?' she said viciously, then grabbed the lead and gave it a harsh tug that had Laura protesting and made her naked breasts sway invitingly. 'Come on then,' Jacqueline added. 'I've got better things to do than waste my time on an ungrateful little slut like you.'

Chapter 25

Laura watched the motorcycles roar off down the drive, with Jacqueline clinging to Zeke's shoulders, her blonde hair flowing out from beneath the helmet. She was relieved to be no longer under the critical eye of the woman, in whose presence she had felt humiliated, intimidated, and ashamed, but as she turned and began collecting the empty and scattered beer cans she longed for a little privacy away from the leering eyes of the few remaining bikers and their two remaining guests.

She went into the kitchen and set about her domestic chores, hoping she would not be missed. Alone in the kitchen she felt momentarily free as she tumbled the clanking cans into a black bin liner, grateful for some solitude at last. But her respite was short-lived, as she soon heard the sound of Jack's bellowing voice.

'Where are you, slave?' he hollered.

Having a fair idea of what sort of things the great ox would demand of her, Laura felt a knot tighten in her stomach and wanted to crawl away and hide somewhere, but dare not. So she hesitantly called back, 'I'm... I'm in the kitchen.'

'Then come out here, and be quick!' came the gruff order.

Laura wondered why she had not agreed to go with the woman. An unexpected opportunity to get away from her torment had presented itself, and she had thrown it away. Not only was she a common slut, as everyone rightly thought of and called her, but she was a foolish slut as well. She was a common, foolish young slut.

Laura blinked as she stepped out from the cool building into the bright sunshine. Tony and Jack were crouched by their motorcycles, tinkering with spanners in hand, still swilling beer. Beside them were Joel and Andrew, neither making any attempt to hide his desire as she appeared.

Jack beckoned to her with an oily hand. 'Come over here,' he said. 'I've got a job for you.' Laura moved closer, eyeing them all suspiciously. 'Andrew here needs to make a call to this place they're going to, to let them know they'll be late arriving.'

Laura could not quite see where things were leading, but knew there would be a twist that would not necessarily be to her liking.

'And I've gone and left the number and my mobile in the car,' Andrew explained, a little unconvincingly.

'So you see the problem,' said Jack. 'We're busy working on our bikes, so you'll have to take them back to the car.'

'M-me?' stammered Laura, although she was hardly surprised by the development, and she gazed across to the distant road. 'But I've...'

'You've what?' Jack challenged.

'I've no clothes on,' she said, rather unnecessarily stating the obvious.

'So what?' Jack chuckled, and Laura's colour deepened, knowing she was not going to be let off the hook.

'I can't walk along the road like this,' she protested with little conviction, glancing down at her bare breasts.

'I don't see why not,' Jack mused. 'Anyhow, you don't have to. From what Andrew's been telling me it seems the car's stopped by the perimeter fence way over there.' He pointed with a spanner. 'You should know enough of the woods by now to lead them there, and there's a gate nearby which isn't locked, so you'll be able to get out to it.'

Laura nodded reluctantly. She had been taken into the woods many times by her captors, and learnt many of the paths that wound through the dense undergrowth. And although she had been told there were some gates that were not necessarily locked, she knew that any attempt to escape would have been futile; even if she managed to get away from the gang, what could she possibly do or where could she possibly go without any clothes?

Jack turned to the men. 'Do you want her to wear the lead?' he asked.

'Will she try to escape?' Andrew asked.

'Nah,' Jack shook his head, sniggering. 'She likes being here too much, don't you, babe?'

Laura said nothing.

'Yeah, go on then,' Andrew said with a clear glint of intent in his eyes, 'indulge us.'

'Can't say as I blame you,' Jack said, with an evident air of respect for the man's response, and then he turned to Laura again. 'So, what are you waiting for? Get a move on.'

Laura reluctantly turned to the two suave businessmen. 'It's this way,' she said, then set off, only too well aware of their eyes on her swaying bottom as she led off towards the woods that fringed the house.

They walked in silence, Andrew holding the lead as the two men flanked the poor girl, who kept her gaze directed to the front, knowing their route would take them through secluded woodland where she would be at their mercy if they decided to try anything on.

But to Laura's immense surprise they did not, and it took them about thirty minutes to reach the fence and then find the nearby gate, just as Jack had said they would. She turned to the men. 'Your car must be somewhere near here,' she told them.

'Really?' Andrew said, seemingly not particularly interested in the news.

'So, shall I take a look?' Joel asked.

'If you like,' Andrew said, his attention on Laura. Joel looked a little puzzled by his colleague's attitude, and then slipped through the gate, leaving them alone, Andrew holding the lead and eyeing her appreciatively while she tried to ignore his attention.

Within a minute Joel was back. 'It's there,' he announced, pointing vaguely. 'A few hundred yards away.'

'Is Jacqueline there?' Andrew asked.

'No, it doesn't look like it. There's nobody about.'

'Then they must have decided they couldn't fix it and gone on to that garage.'

'I suppose so,' Joel agreed. 'So, are we going to get your phone?'

'You can go for it if you like,' Andrew said.

'But...' Joel started.

Andrew looked at him despairingly. 'And how are we going to get into the car?' he asked rhetorically. 'Jacqueline has the key.'

Joel looked puzzled again. 'Oh,' he said, 'so...?' and then he stopped with his mouth open as though catching flies as Andrew slowly produced his mobile from a trouser pocket.

Both Laura and Joel stared at him. 'What?' they echoed.

'Well, I had to get this little beauty away from those cretins up at the house,' he explained, answering their unspoken question, smiling broadly with smug satisfaction that his scheme was working so well. 'And they inadvertently did the tricky part by getting Jacqueline out of the way. I thought that was extremely hospitable of them.'

Joel shook his head. 'I don't believe this,' he said.

Andrew, shifting his gaze to his colleague pulled Laura closer with the lead, and reached out and cupped the underside of one of her firm breasts. He held it, his hand not moving, as though putting it on display for the other man. 'Don't you think she's lovely?' he asked, and then, not needing confirmation of the other man's opinion on her beauty, went on, 'So why don't we indulge ourselves a little, mm? We have some time on our hands, we have some privacy, and thanks to my ingenuity, we have the girl.'

Laura closed her eyes and her shoulders slumped. She had known all along that if the two wanted her she had no choice but to surrender to their demands. And now, her suspicions were proving well founded.

'Come on,' said Andrew, breaking into her thoughts. 'Get on your knees and suck me.' He tugged on the lead, jerking her down, and opening his trousers he pulled out his thick, stiff cock.

Without waiting to hear any further demands, knowing resistance was futile, Laura leant closer and took him into her mouth.

'That's better,' he gasped, one hand dropping to her head and guiding her gently back and forth. 'Suck and enjoy.' He looked at the other man. 'Come on Joel,' he urged. 'Come and have some fun. She loves it.'

'She might, and so would I,' said Joel. 'But what about Jacqueline? She'd kill me if she found out.'

'To hell with Jacqueline,' Andrew said scornfully, his hips stabbing at the face buried against his groin. 'Come and have some fun. Look, how cute is her arse? And I know how much you love a cute arse.'

There was a pause in the debate, Andrew's final words seeming to hold great sway, then Laura felt hands grasping her buttocks and pulling them apart and something bulbous and stiff prising its way into her anus, her cries muffled by a mouthful of cock as Joel eased his way deep inside her.

He buggered her with gusto, shunting her body back and forth, her stretched lips sliding up and down Andrew's shaft as she continued to obediently suck him.

The sight of her sandwiched between them on her hands and knees was too much for the pair, because it was only a matter of a few minutes of hectic rutting before she heard strangled groans of ecstasy and her mouth filled with hot, salty semen, and moments later her bottom was similarly anointed...

'And what the fuck's going on here?!'

At first Laura was barely aware of the voice, but then she felt Joel's shrinking penis being snatched from between her buttocks and knew something was very wrong. She drew her head back, letting Andrew's wilting shaft slip from between her lips, then gazed up.

An icy chill gripped her.

It was Jacqueline, towering over her, glaring down upon her shame.

Chapter 26

As Laura trudged back through the woods she reflected on the injustice of her situation. Her lead was held firmly in one hand by Jacqueline, who jerked it violently every time she showed any sign of lagging.

Behind her walked a shamefaced Joel, Andrew having been despatched to drive the repaired car back to the house. Laura could scarcely credit her bad luck that, while she was at the mercy of the two men, the bikers and Jacqueline had passed by, noticed the open gate, and investigated to see if any unwelcome visitors were intruding. If only she had heard the bikes approaching things might have been all right. As it was, however, the haughty woman was far from amused.

Zeke it was who had pulled poor Laura to her feet, trapping her hands behind her while Jacqueline unleashed her considerable venom on her two companions, cuffing both across the face while the humbled pair tucked their shrinking penises back into their trousers.

When she finished with them Jacqueline turned on Laura, slapping the helpless girl as she launched a tirade of abuse upon her. Laura tried to protest her innocence, but she couldn't deny that when Jacqueline had discovered them, there had been no disguising her own passion as she gave herself to the rutting pair.

Now, as they were making their way back to the house, Laura knew that Jacqueline had some kind of punishment in store for her, and her heart thumped as she tried to imagine what it might be. There was a cruel air about the woman that Laura had seen from the start, and she knew that, naked and vulnerable as she was, she could expect no mercy.

What she could not comprehend was the sense of excitement she felt as she trudged through the woods. She should be begging for mercy, but the prospect of what was to come was already stirring her to new levels of arousal. Why should the prospect of further humiliation and pain make her feel such a way? She glanced down at her breasts, and was dismayed to see how her nipples protruded, puckered and erect. Was there no limit to her licentiousness?

As they rounded the last bend in the track that ran up to the house, Laura's face fell. The row of bikes told her that the rest of the gang had returned. As usual they were all lounging about, as ribald as ever and swilling beer earnestly, and Laura gasped with dismay as she realised that, whatever form her punishment was destined to take, it would be witnessed by all of them.

As she was led amongst the group Georgie stepped forward to meet her. 'Been putting it about again, I hear,' she said.

'And that's not all that's going to happen to the little whore,' Jacqueline promised sharply.

Georgie eyed the newcomer with interest. 'You going to thrash her?' she asked.

'I am,' Jacqueline declared imperiously. 'After all, I caught the little trollop with my man.'

Georgie shook her head with amusement. 'She can't get enough of it, that's her trouble. Want to get her cleaned up first?'

'Yes I do, and somebody get me some rope.'

Before she could protest in any way Laura was lifted bodily, and once again forced to suffer the indignity of being plunged in the pond. By the time it was decreed that she was sufficiently clean and she stood on the lawn, wet and shivering, someone had found a rope and given it to Jacqueline. It was coarse, and it bit into her tender flesh as the woman bound her elbows and then her wrists together behind her back, heedless to her cries of anguish. Once she was helpless, Jacqueline pushed her across to a nearby tree.

With the audience lazing back and admiring Jacqueline's domineering performance she threw the rope over a branch and began to haul, pulling Laura's arms up painfully behind her and forcing her to bend forward. She pulled until Laura felt certain her arms would be pulled from their sockets, and then fastened the end of the rope to the trunk. As she was doing so, Georgie was driving two stakes into the earth about a yard apart on either side of the trussed girl's feet. Once they were firmly in place she took two shorter lengths of rope and bound Laura's ankles to the stakes, forcing her legs apart.

Laura found herself in the most uncomfortable and degrading position imaginable, her body bent forward, her legs spread, her firm breasts swaying as she breathed. The strain on her sinews was intense, and she bit her lip as she tried her best to ignore the aching in her arms and shoulders.

Something hard touched her face and she raised her eyes to see Jacqueline standing in front of her. The woman was holding a long thin cane, and a shiver ran through Laura's body as she felt it rub her cheek.

'Now I'm going to show you what happens to a little tart who touches my man,' growled Jacqueline. 'A few fresh stripes across your backside will teach you a lesson you won't forget in a hurry, believe me.'

Then, to Laura's surprise, the woman began to undo her blouse, quickly unfastening the buttons, then shrugging the garment off and dropping it to the ground. Underneath she wore a black bra that lifted and squeezed her large breasts. Amid whistles from the watching bikers she then dropped her hands to her waist and unzipped her slacks. She slipped them off too, revealing a pair of matching black briefs that were cut high at the hip and dropped to a V between her thighs.

Jacqueline turned to the grinning bikers, clearly confident to be so scantily dressed and proud of her impressive body. Laura could see Joel staring at her in impotent fury, and she knew the display was as much to annoy him as it was to satisfy Jacqueline's own comfort and exhibitionist tendencies. Then her attention was drawn back to the cane as the woman swept it down through the air.

Jacqueline moved round behind the helpless girl and Laura felt the cane tap against her bottom, and a cold chill ran through her as Jacqueline sadistically ran its thin length across her bare, vulnerable flesh.

The woman rapped the cane twice more against the tight skin of Laura's bottom, and then she drew back her arm.

Swish! *Whack*!

It came down hard across her tender, unprotected buttocks, the whippy tip wrapping around the smooth contours while the pain coursed through her body, making her scream aloud.

Swish! *Whack*!

A second stripe was cut across the pale skin of Laura's haunches, the cane slicing into her and doubling the agony.

Swish! *Whack*!

Again the cane fell, finding a new area of Laura's bottom and decorating it with another thin white stripe that darkened almost immediately to an angry red.

Swish! *Whack*!
Swish! *Whack*!
Swish! *Whack*!

Laura was howling now, writhing in a desperate and fruitless attempt to avoid the cane as it lashed down.

Swish! *Whack*!
Swish! *Whack*!
Swish! *Whack*!

Jacqueline showed no mercy to the weeping girl, wielding the cane with all her might and expertise. Laura's body was coated in sweat, the tears rolling down her cheeks as the woman continued to lay stripe after stripe across her stinging bottom.

Swish! *Whack*!
Swish! *Whack*!
Swish! *Whack*!

Then, at last, Jacqueline lowered the cane, wiping beads of perspiration from her forehead with her forearm. For a few moments there was silence, broken only by Laura's sobs as she writhed in her bonds, her bottom on fire. So intense was the pain that she barely registered what was happening when Jacqueline took hold of her hair and dragged her face up to stare into her own.

'I don't think you'll be touching my man again, will you?'

Laura shook her head, blinking through the blur of her tears.

Satisfied, Jacqueline turned away from her and made her way across to where Joel was standing. She grasped his shirt and pulled him against her, planting her lips on his and kissing him passionately. He reached for her, his hand closing over her bra. The kiss went on for a full minute, and then she pushed him away.

'What I need is a *real* man,' she sneered, reaching back and unclipping her bra.

'What the...?' gasped Joel. 'Not here, Jacks.'

'And why not?' she retorted tartly. 'Here's as good a place as any. And besides, I don't think you're in any position to be telling me what I can and can't do. Now why don't you just be quiet, lest I get *really* angry?'

She undid the clip and the bra fell to the ground. A gasp went up around the bikers as she bared her breasts. They were magnificent, large and firm with big, brown areolae and protruding nipples. Once again Joel protested as she reached for her panties, but she ignored him, slipping them off and kicking them aside. Her pubic bush was blonde, like her hair, her thick sex lips visible beneath.

'Christ, I need a cock,' she declared brazenly.

Joel took a step towards her but she turned away from him to where Leo was standing, took hold of his hand and placed it on her breast. 'You want to fuck me?' she purred.

Leo grinned and pulled her to him. 'Sure,' he said, 'I want to fuck you.'

'Now just you wait a minute...' Joel protested impotently, but fell quiet as Leo turned on him aggressively.

'What's your problem?' he snarled, and Joel backed away, saying nothing more, looking clumsy and foolish.

'If you want to fuck something again, use the slut,' Jacqueline spat maliciously, indicating poor Laura. Then she took Leo's hand and led him to the house, amid murmurs of approval from the other bikers. Joel simply stood, staring powerlessly after them.

For a moment nobody moved. Then Jack rose to his feet. 'Hell, if you don't want her, there's plenty here that do,' he declared.

He strolled across to where Laura was tied, unbuttoning his fly as he went. Laura saw his stiff erection spring into view, and a sudden shudder of arousal ran through her bound frame. Despite the dreadful pain of the beating, she realised with a shock that her predicament had once again aroused her most perverse desires, and she felt her vagina contract with anticipation as Jack moved round behind her.

There was a pause, then he thrust his rigid cock into her and began pounding back and forth, shoving against her body and reminding her of the pain in her shoulders and wrists. He fucked her with vigour, making her breasts shudder and drawing cries of pleasure from her.

When she felt his cock erupting she came too, moaning aloud at the release of her orgasm. Then he had withdrawn and Tony's penis was invading her while others stood watching, their erections in their fists, waiting their turn.

Laura wasn't sure how many times she was fucked that afternoon, but her orgasms became more and more intense as she surrendered to their aggressive dominance and her own lustful desires. Eventually they cut her down, leaving her legs tied to the stakes as they took her at will.

By evening the men were spent and Laura was left alone, exhausted, sprawled flat on the grass.

She was awoken by a shake, and stared up uncomprehendingly, blinking into the large, red, evening sun.

'Wh-what is it?' she started.

'Come on, it's time to go home,' said Cassandra.

Chapter 27

Laura shook her head, trying to gather her thoughts. 'But I don't understand,' she said. 'Why did you want to take it out on me? What harm have I ever done you?'

'I don't know,' replied Cassandra, placing a hand on the girl's shoulder. 'I just wanted to get back at Sir John.'

The pair were in Laura's bedroom, the girl stretched out on her bed in her underwear, while the housekeeper sat beside her. It was three days since Laura had been released from the clutches of the bikers. She had slept for twenty-four hours after her return, and then allowed the woman to bathe her and to rub soothing ointments into the marks of her punishment. By the time her guardian arrived back from his holiday that afternoon she was almost fully recovered from her ordeal, and ate dinner with him that evening.

After the meal she excused herself and returned to the sanctuary of her room, only to find Cassandra waiting there for her, and was struck at once by the woman's serious expression.

'What is it?' she asked. 'Is something the matter?'

And then it all came out; Cassandra told her about her father, and about how he had been unfairly dismissed from the household. She went on to confess to the girl her desire for revenge, explaining how she had intended to expose his young ward's promiscuity to him - and to the press.

'But it's not as if he and I are fond of one another,' said Laura. 'He just keeps me here out of a sense of duty.'

'Yes, I know,' Cassandra conceded, nodding her agreement. 'But a scandal could have ruined him, and I guess that's what I wanted.'

Laura reached for the housekeeper's hand. 'I suppose he did treat your father very badly,' she said with genuine sympathy.

'He did, but that was no reason to take it out on you. I was spiteful and wrong.'

'Well, at least I know the truth now,' Laura said, with a degree of understanding that only increased the expression of guilt on Cassandra's face. 'And I'm just glad you told me.'

The older woman smiled. 'And I'm glad I stopped it before it could get any further out of hand. I just didn't expect you to respond the way you did.'

Laura's face reddened. 'Neither did I. You seem to have found something inside me that I didn't know about myself. Do you think I'm some kind of nymphomaniac?'

Cassandra smiled. 'I suppose you might be.'

'So what should I do about it?'

'I'm not sure. Live with it, I guess. Enjoy it. It seems a shame to suppress your true nature.'

'I'm not sure I could suppress it, now you've shown me what I'm capable of.'

'You really love giving yourself, don't you?'

'Yes.' Laura's colour deepened and she lowered her eyes. 'I just want to submit to people's demands. Is that awful?'

Cassandra leaned forward and gently kissed Laura on the lips.

'We all have our desires,' she said. 'Yours are just a little more extreme than most, that's all.'

'The trouble is, I'm trapped in this place,' said Laura. 'Now Sir John's back I'll have to return to being the obedient and innocent ward.'

'I'll try to help you,' said Cassandra. She slipped a hand under Laura's bra and closed it over the softness of her breast, bringing a sigh from the girl. 'While I'm still here, that is,' she added.

Laura's eyes widened. 'What does that mean?' she asked.

'Well, the truth is that I've decided to move on. There's no point staying here, bearing a grudge like I have been. It's time to make a fresh start.'

'But what will you do?'

'I've been offered a job at that club I took you to.'

'The one where I was first beaten?'

'That's right. They need a full-time manageress, and I guess I was kind of cut out for the role.'

Laura squeezed the woman's hand. 'I wish I could come with you.'

Cassandra smiled. 'I bet most of the customers feel the same. You could come over some evenings, when you can get away. I'm sure you'd be a huge attraction.'

A thrill of excitement ran through Laura's body as she remembered her night at the club. 'I think I'd like that,' she said. 'But still, it's going to be awful without you here.'

Cassandra leaned closer and kissed the girl again, her hand squeezing and caressing the softness of her breast. Laura responded by slipping an arm around her neck, her tongue probing tentatively into the woman's mouth as a wave of desire swept through her.

The housekeeper moved her other hand lower, running it over Laura's belly and slipping her fingers under the waistband of the girl's brief panties, and Laura sighed as Cassandra found her clitoris. 'Mmm,' she murmured.

At that moment a bell sounded somewhere below and Cassandra stiffened, reluctantly pulling her lips from Laura's. 'What on earth can he want at this time?' she said in frustration, rising from the bed and smoothing down her black dress.

Laura gave a little sigh of disappointment. 'You won't be long, will you?'

'That depends on what Sir John needs me for. He doesn't usually call me at this time.'

Laura watched the woman leave, then lay back. Cassandra's caresses had ignited her needs, and for a moment she was sorely tempted to touch herself to quell her excitement, but then she decided to wait for Cassandra's return.

Five minutes later the housekeeper did return. 'Hi,' smiled Laura, stretching her lovely body. 'I was thinking we could...' Her voice trailed away as she saw the pale colour of Cassandra's cheeks. 'Is something wrong?' she asked anxiously.

'Put your dress on, Laura,' Cassandra said seriously, her tone flat. 'You've got to come downstairs with me.'

'But why?' Laura asked, feeling decidedly unsettled by the woman's changed and distant demeanour. 'What's happened? Why are you looking like that?'

'Just come down with me,' Cassandra insisted, giving nothing away.

Laura rose from her bed. She had draped her dress over a chair, so she picked it up and slipped it on.

'Come on,' said the housekeeper.

'But what is it, Cassandra?' Laura tried again. 'What's upset you?'

But Cassandra said nothing as she led the way downstairs with Laura close behind. The girl's stomach was a tight knot as she tried to fathom the housekeeper's sudden and extreme change of mood. They stopped outside Sir John's study, and the woman knocked lightly.

'Come!'

Laura followed Cassandra into the room and then came to an abrupt halt, the blood draining from her face as she took in the scene. Sir John was standing beside his desk, looking extremely stern. Beside him, sitting in his leather chair, was another figure.

It was Jacqueline.

Laura could scarcely believe her eyes as she stared at the woman. She was dressed as elegantly as ever, an inscrutable smile on her face as she watched the youngster's reaction to her presence.

'Ah, here she is,' Jacqueline purred. 'She looks a little different with her clothes on, but that's her all right.'

'That will do, Miss Kurwen,' Sir John said to Cassandra, dismissing her.

Laura glanced beseechingly at the housekeeper. The last thing she wanted was to be left alone with her guardian and the severe woman, but she knew Cassandra had to obey her employer. As she left, Cassandra managed to transmit a faint smile of reassurance to the tremulous girl.

The door closed, and Sir John glared at Laura. 'Do you know this lady?' he asked.

Feeling too ill at ease to speak, Laura nodded mutely.

'I think you must, because it would appear she knows you extremely well,' he went on. 'She's been telling me some extraordinary tales concerning you. Now, let's hear what you have to say for yourself.'

'Yes, little slut,' Jacqueline hissed. 'Tell your guardian what you've been up to for the last couple of weeks.'

It was nearly an hour later when Laura finally returned to her room. Her face was ashen, and there were tearstains meandering down her cheeks. Cassandra was waiting for her, sitting on the edge of the bed, her expression grim.

'Are you all right?' she asked.

'I... I think so,' Laura said quietly, unable to believe what was happening.

'What went on down there?'

Laura sat down beside the housekeeper, utterly crestfallen. 'Oh, Cassandra, it was simply awful,' she said, and went on to relate how Jacqueline had described to her guardian her internment at the hands of the bikers, how she had been brazenly naked and had given herself without question to anyone who wanted her, and then made Laura show Sir John the fading stripes on her bottom.

'But why has she done all this?' asked Cassandra.

'Because I let her boyfriend fool around with me,' said Laura. 'Evidently a thoroughly sadistic caning wasn't enough. When she realised who I was the spiteful cow decided upon even more revenge. Apparently Andrew recognised me from some PR event I went to last year with Sir John, and as soon as she found out she just couldn't wait to come and tell him everything.'

'So what's he going to do now?'

'Oh, Cassandra, you wouldn't believe it,' Laura wailed.

'Tell me.'

'Apparently he has a cousin who runs some kind of religious commune on some remote northern island.'

'A religious commune?' Cassandra echoed warily. 'What kind of a religious commune?'

'Apparently it's like a sort of nunnery,' Laura told her. 'All sackcloth and ashes, living a frugal life of contemplation and prayer, and he wants them to take me in until my inheritance comes through.'

'But, that's two years away,' Cassandra said, aghast.

'I know; two years living in a cell on some bleak island in the middle of nowhere surrounded by nothing but hostile seas.' Laura was desperate. 'I'll go mad, Cassandra. This can't be happening to me!'

The housekeeper shook her head pensively. 'Well then, we just can't let it happen,' she decided.

'But I can't see what choice I have,' Laura lamented. 'He's sent me up here to pack. There's nowhere I can go to get away...'

'There might be one place...' Cassandra said slowly. 'There just might be one place.'

Chapter 28

'Look, Laura, are you absolutely certain you want to go through with this?' Cassandra asked one last time.

'Yes, Cassandra, I want to do it,' the girl said adamantly.

'But it might be dangerous.'

'I hope it is. Remember, the alternative is two years' incarceration in some hostile place in the middle of the sea somewhere. Besides which, you know these people and what they're capable of. It was you who left me with them in the first place, and this was originally your idea.'

Cassandra sighed. 'You're right,' she relented. 'They're a rough lot, but they do look after their own kind.'

'And that's exactly what I'd be; one of their own kind,' Laura said pluckily. 'Come on, Cassandra, let's go before I do change my mind.'

Laura gazed ahead through the windscreen of Cassandra's car. They were parked in a lay-by close to the diner where the bikers hung out. She could see the neon signs, and the shadowy figures of some bikers as they stood around their powerful machines outside. Now she simply wanted to get there, and to carry out the plan.

Her inheritance, she knew, was safe. It was simply a case of how she spent the two years before it became due to her, and she was certain that living the life of a nun in an oppressive religious retreat in the middle of nowhere was not something she would be able to tolerate for very long, if at all.

It had been relatively simple to sneak out of her guardian's house. Such was his confidence that he would be obeyed in all matters, he hadn't thought to lock the door of her room, simply sending her there with instructions to be packed and ready to leave in the morning. She had waited in bed for an hour, until the house was completely quiet, then dressed and crept to Cassandra's room.

So Cassandra had driven her through the darkened lanes, then stopped and checked for a final time that this was what Laura really wanted. Now she slipped the car into gear and they cruised the last few hundred yards into the brash lights thrown out by the diner.

Even before the car came to a halt Laura spotted Georgie, talking to a group of men, some of whom she recognised from her previous visits. Eyes turned in their direction as they climbed from the vehicle, and Georgie sauntered over.

'Hi, Cassandra,' she said, and then turned to Laura. 'I didn't expect to see you back here,' she remarked.

'I... I want to talk to Spanner,' stammered the young beauty, immediately unnerved by the presence of the overbearing girl biker.

Georgie laughed. 'Don't tell me you've decided to become his chattel!'

Laura hesitated, took a deep breath, glanced anxiously at Cassandra for a moment, and then said, 'Yes, that's exactly what I've decided.'

Georgie stared at her for a moment, and then gave a low whistle. 'Are you serious?' she said.

'Perfectly serious,' Laura insisted. 'Is he here?'

'Sure, he's here,' the biker confirmed, and then turned to Cassandra and asked, 'Is this on the level?'

Cassandra nodded. 'It's on the level. Why, don't you think Laura's up to it?'

Georgie shook her head. 'No, I've never met anyone more suited.' She looked into Laura's eyes. 'I was a chattel once, you know,' she disclosed.

'You? But I thought...'

'And you're going to have to get used to taking orders,' Georgie cut across her, 'and to wearing only what you're told to wear. So take your dress off; it's what Spanner will expect.'

Laura hesitated, the blood rising to her cheeks. Then she slowly shrugged out of her dress, aware that all eyes were on her clad only in bra and panties, then handed the flimsy garment to Cassandra.

Georgie ran her eyes up and down Laura's shapely frame, and then nodded. 'Come on, then,' she said. 'Let's go meet lover boy.'

The inside of the diner was warm and smoky as always, the scents and sounds immediately reminding Laura of her period of enslavement by the bikers. Far from discouraging her, however, she found herself suddenly overwhelmed by an intense sexual arousal as she felt the many eyes staring at her from around the room. She looked about, then gave a little shudder as she recognised the craggy features of Spanner across the room.

Georgie led her to him. He was speaking to a biker Laura hadn't seen before, who ogled her appreciatively as she approached.

'So, what have we here?' the stranger drawled.

'The slut wants to talk to Spanner,' said Georgie.

The big biker fixed his familiar eyes on Laura, and the sight of him again made her knees weaken. 'Yeah, what is it?' he said with little apparent interest.

Laura looked round at Cassandra, then took a deep breath. 'Remember what you were saying about chattels?' she said quietly.

'Yeah, of course,' he confirmed, with a terse nod of his head.

'Well, that's what I want to be,' she blurted clumsily. 'I want to be your chattel.'

Annoyingly, he showed no surprise, his only physical reaction being a slight, wry smile. 'I knew you would,' he said, and then turned to Cassandra. 'You in on this?' he asked.

Cassandra nodded, and then gave him a brief rundown of Laura's situation.

'And you're sure this guardian bloke won't come after her, or try to cause trouble for us?' he asked warily once she had concluded.

'He might try, but there's not much he can do. After all, she's of age. Besides, he won't want to risk a scandal. As long as she's kept out of the way and doesn't endanger his position, it'll be no problem.'

'Okay,' said Spanner, 'I'll take her. But first she has to have my mark. Take her and get it done, Georgie.'

The girl biker nodded, then took Laura's arm. 'Come on,' she said.

Laura was only too aware of the eyes watching her as she was led across the room once more and out of the front door. She glanced back nervously at Cassandra, who was already deep in conversation with Spanner. Georgie took her out and past a line of motorcycles to a small shack next-door, one that Laura had barely noticed before.

Georgie pushed open the door and led the girl inside. The interior was brightly lit, and a man sat beside a low leather couch. He wore black, and had orange spiky hair. There was a ring through his nose that glinted in the light. He eyed Laura speculatively.

'Got a job for you, Chuck,' said Georgie. 'Spanner's got himself a chattel.'

The man's eyebrows lifted. 'A chattel?' he echoed. 'Haven't done one of them for a while. Spanner, you say?'

'That's right. You know what's needed?'

'Sure,' he said dismissively. 'Come here, darlin'.' He beckoned to Laura.

She moved nervously forward, a little unsure of what form Spanner's mark would take. She was concerned about the idea, but at the same time enormously excited by the prospect of bearing a mark of ownership, thus making her a true slave.

'Take your knickers off and lie face down,' ordered the man, indicating the couch.

Laura gazed anxiously about. There were two other bikers in the room, browsing some tattoo designs, but they looked up and watched avidly as the blushing girl reached for the waistband of her panties. She pulled them down in a single movement, and then quickly lay on the couch, shivering slightly at the sensation of the smooth leather on her bare flesh.

Chuck busied himself with some equipment, then sat down beside her, holding a pen-shaped tool in his hand, and ran his fingers over the smooth flesh of her bare buttock.

'This will prick a little bit,' he said, and then switched on the device, and Laura felt the sharp sting of a needle penetrating her flesh.

Chuck worked fast and expertly, humming to himself as he perfected the design. Laura let herself relax, scarcely feeling the needle as he worked. It took him about ten minutes, after which he switched off the pen.

'What do you think?' he asked Georgie.

'Nice job, Chuck,' the biker girl said, despite looking somewhat bored. 'Show her.'

Chuck took Laura's arm and raised her from the couch. The two onlookers' eyes bulged eagerly, and once again Laura felt her face glowing as she stood in front of them, naked apart from her bra. Chuck took her across to a full-length mirror on one wall.

'Take a look,' he said.

Laura turned and glanced back over her shoulder. The design was a simple one; a blue spanner with red ivy leaves wrapped about it. It was not much more than an inch across, set high on her right buttock where it would just be covered by her panties. There was something extremely sexy about the mark - something that brought a knot of excitement to the girl's stomach.

'You're really Spanner's now,' Georgie announced, and Laura nodded, still scarcely able to believe what she had done. 'Come on, Laura. I'll take you back.'

The girl stared at Georgie; it was the first time the biker had ever referred to her by name, and she felt a strange warmth deep inside. Despite her lowly status, Georgie was actually recognising her as part of the bikers' world.

She put her panties back on, careful not to let the delicate material touch her new tattoo, and Georgie led her back into the diner. Spanner was standing where she had left him, still with Cassandra.

'So, are you marked?' he asked, straight to the point as ever.

Laura nodded meekly.

'Show me,' he said. 'Take everything off.'

Laura hesitated for a second, glanced around the crowded diner, then at Cassandra, and then back at her new master.

She reached back and unclipped her bra. For a second she held it to her breasts, then, her cheeks glowing, she let it drop to the floor. Her hands were shaking slightly as she grasped her panties and pulled them down and off, and then she looked deep into Spanner's eyes.

He walked slowly around her, fingering near his mark of ownership, careful not to touch it. The room was silent now and Laura stood motionless, trembling as he inspected her naked form, and the sensation sent spasms of excitement coursing through her.

'You're my chattel now,' he said quietly. 'And your duty is to please me.'

Laura could not speak, and so she nodded humbly.

'You'll do what I say? Obey every order?'

Again she nodded.

'Very good.' He seemed pleased, and that secretly thrilled her. 'You see that table over there?' he went on.

Laura glanced in the direction he was indicating. About six bikers were lounging back, their eyes fixed on her. She nodded.

'You're going to fuck all six of 'em, little chattel,' he decreed. 'Right here, right now, in front of all my friends. Do you understand?'

Such was the overwhelming cocktail of mixed emotions swamping Laura that she thought she might faint there and then, but managed to mumble, 'Yes... I understand.'

'Good.'

Then, to her dismay, Spanner turned his back on her and casually ordered a fresh coffee. She glanced nervously across at the designated group slouched around the table, then made her way over to them. Everybody was watching her; apart, it seemed, from the one person she wanted to watch her - Spanner.

Eventually she reached the table. The man closest to her was balding and overweight. Saying nothing, and with no further backward glances at her new owner, Laura dropped to her knees. She reached for the man's fly, tugged it down and fumbled inside, worming her trembling fingers into his briefs and releasing a long, circumcised cock, which was already stiffening under her cool touch. Bravely, without hesitation, she leant forward, took him into her mouth, and began sucking with as much enthusiasm as she could muster.

His penis hardened instantly, filling her mouth as he pressed his groin up against her flushed face, and despite her predicament Laura was instantly aroused by the scent and feel of his rampant stalk, forgetting momentarily the exhibition she was making of herself, her breasts quivering deliciously as she worked her head up and down.

Then he was grasping her hair and pulling her face up from his lap. She looked at him with wide eyes, wondering what was expected of her next.

'I want a fuck,' he grunted.

Aided by the brutish fingers entwined in her hair Laura rose to her feet, and he reached out and fingered her crudely, probing into the heat of her vagina and drawing an instinctive moan of pleasure from her lips.

'She wants it bad, boys,' he announced to his watching friends.

'Yeah, and I'll have some too,' remarked one of them, loosening his gaudy belt buckle.

'You can all have me,' Laura said quietly, glancing sideways at Spanner. Then she lifted a leg and straddled the fat biker's lap, facing him, her breasts moulding to his avaricious face. She lowered herself gently, grasping his cock and guiding it into her wet vagina, barely stifling a moan as she dropped down and he filled her completely. Once he was buried within her she began to move, rising and falling, her milky breasts juddering as she fucked him earnestly.

Through half-closed, misty eyes she saw them all watching her, scarcely able to believe her own lasciviousness. This would be her life from now on, she told herself. Not for her the modesty of clothes or the option to choose her partner. She was a chattel now, a biker's whore, a sex slave under the power of Spanner, or anyone else he decided to give her to. Her duty was to pleasure men and women in any way she was told, to anyone who wanted to sample her charms.

As these thoughts passed through her mind a powerful orgasm suddenly shook her body, and she cried aloud with the intense pleasure of it.

This truly was, Laura knew, sweet submission.

Innocent and in trouble!

Enjoy more damsel in distress erotic adventures by Lia Anderssen in **Total Abandon**, also available as a paperback at **AMAZON**...

She tried to struggle, but once again the strength of the two was too much for her and she had no chance. They worked quickly, clearly used to using the equipment. Danni's hands were pulled above her head and cold metal manacles closed about her wrists. Once these were in place the pair did the same with her legs, ignoring her desperate protests, closing the steel bands about her ankles and holding her fast. She was immobilised now, but still they hadn't finished. Taking hold of the chains, they hauled on them, pulling them tight and stretching Danni's lovely young body into the shape of an X.

Danni tugged at her bonds, but in vain. She was quite unable to move, her slender limbs pulled tight and already beginning to ache. On the wall directly opposite the frame was a mirror. With a groan of despair she closed her eyes against the sight of her own stretched and vulnerable body.

When sexually innocent Danni Bright takes a lift from a stranger, she gets more than she bargained for. Left alone and naked in an hotel bedroom she falls into the hands of gangsters, who use her in all sorts of wicked and erotic ways.

Forced to sell her body on the street, bound and whipped by a whore, made to dance naked for the customers in a seedy bar and then to work as a lap-dancer in a cheap club, she slowly begins to come to terms with her sexuality.

But serious villains are after her, and the young beauty experiences a great deal of pleasure and pain before her story is over.